A SHORT STAY IN HELL

A SHORT STAY IN HELL

Steven L. Peck

ఆ STRANGE VIOLIN EDITIONS ಶಿ
WASHINGTON, DC

FIRST EDITION, MARCH 2012
Copyright © 2012 by Steven L. Peck

Strange Violin Editions
4200 Cathedral Avenue, NW, #702
Washington, DC 20016
http://strangeviolineditions.com

ISBN 978-0-9837484-2-7
ISBN 978-0-9837484-4-1 (hardcover)
ISBN 978-0-9837484-3-4 (e-book)

Library of Congress Control Number: 2011941923

Printed in the United States of America

PROLOGUE

Although I have loved many, there has been only one genuine love in my near-eternally stretched life — Rachel who fell to the bottom of the library without me. Did I know her only for so short a time? Strange, how a moment of existence can cut so deeply into our being that while ages pass unnoticed, a brief love can structure and define the very topology of our consciousness ever after. I'm getting ahead of myself. I suppose I must start at the beginning — a beginning so long ago that its horizon is a vanishing point at the convergence of two Euclidian lines that would be parallel by any human measure.

The first years are the easiest to describe. They were years of adventure, companionship, and love. I have not seen anyone for uncountable years. Yet, even after so long, I still listen for the sound of another's voice, the ring of footsteps on the stairs, or a figure moving silhouetted in the distance. Once I spent a year just listening. Another, trying to build a telescope made from clarified sheep intestines from the kiosk, so that I might look deep into the library. Despite my substantial efforts, I have failed to find another soul. We have all scattered far and wide into the vastness of this space and cannot find one another. I suspect by now we are all alone.

Yet I labor on. By my count (which I know is accurate, for my memory in this place, it seems, is incapable of forgetting even the smallest detail) I have climbed innumerable light-years, from the lowest level to this one where I sit with this book in my hands reading of my stay here. It is not the story of my life, so it serves little purpose, but as I read I marvel that I've found such a book. It is close to the one I seek. Sometimes I fantasize I will discover the book that describes the location of the volume I have been searching for. But alas, how would I know it was the right one? There are countless books in the library that claim a particular floor contains the one I need. And then, of course, no single book could contain a number so large that the height and depth of this library could be expressed as a numerical digit. Silly thoughts in this monotonous place are inevitable I suppose.

I have found many treasures. A couple of eons ago I found a book that looked like it described my earthly digestive history—from beginning to end, every meal, how the food was broken into its chemical composition and then sent on to the intestine. I've also grown fond of what I'm sure are very close to Mickey Spillane novels. So, too, I remember that for about seven hundred billion years I carried a book of short stories—some were fantasies, some romances, and one was a farce. It was a marvelous book. The last story was my favorite. It told of a monkey, once the powerful owner of a lawnmower repair business, who falls into obscurity and despair. It told of his sorrow at having lost his greatness and reputation in the field as technological changes outstripped his ability to keep up. He spoke movingly of his search for religion. I still get teary-eyed when I think of the ending of that story (which I won't spoil by telling you).

One book I found not long ago was full of random characters except for pages 111 to 222, wherein I found an exposition that speculated that God had created the universe as a way of sorting through the great library, finding those books that were most beautiful and meaningful. It argued that in the mere sixteen billion years of my old universe's existence, a vast store of great thought and literature had been produced during the short creative life of human existence on the planet. The work entertained the notion that evolution was the most effective sorting algorithm for finding the subsets of coherent and readable books that are scattered thinly throughout the randomness of the library. The argument took on special meaning to me because it had been almost 160 billion years since I had found such a long string of coherent text. To find such a delightful work was a treasure indeed — especially such a germane treatise nestled between such auspicious page numbers.

Forgive me. I'm getting far ahead of myself. I must start at the beginning if there is to be any hope that you might understand my life in Hell and the fateful day the great demon sent me here.

I must start with the interview or none of this will make sense. So I begin here:

THE PROFICIENT DEMON leaned back comfortably in his large, high-backed red leather chair, then swung away from the five terrified guests seated before him and turned to the window behind him. The room was well lit, with long incandescent tubes arranged in several functional pairs that spanned the length of the ceiling, giving the room a soft, businesslike feel. Potted plants, placed tastefully here and there, lent the room a sense of proportion and order. The demon was the only thing that did not seem to belong.

The monster's yellow gaze was directed thoughtfully out of the large framed window that dominated the wall behind his desk. Behind the glass was a large cavern lit with a dancing red glow. He sighed and scratched his leg with one of his black-tipped hooves as he surveyed the seething, molten bed of lava, bubbling thickly like slowly boiling sweet candy syrup in the scene below him. Occasionally from the lake of fire a blazing fountain would erupt violently, spackling the ceiling of the great cavern with hot lava, which then would drip in large globs slowly back to the enormous magma lake, creating high, thick splashes of bright orange liquid rock. Inside the lake, scores of wailing people could be seen wading through the pool, screaming in agony, and even though their cries could not pierce the thickness of the glass window, the muted agony and terror visible on their faces transferred the terror of the situation to the five seated guests. All five were trembling and breathless.

On the lake's edge, small shadowy demons wielded jagged leather whips and long rusted pitchforks to drive those souls desperately trying to scramble out of the pool back to its bubbling center. The yellow-eyed demon swiveled back toward the three men and two women staring back at him wide-eyed with horror. They were dressed simply in thick white robes of rough cotton. Their feet were bare and they were seated on unstable gray metal folding chairs that squeaked loudly whenever they moved.

The imposing demon was tall — about eight feet. His large goat legs sported coarse, thick hair, giving him a satyr-like aspect without the charm of a classical Pan. His torso was exceptionally well muscled, fire engine–red like his face, but covered with a thin layer of moisture from which seemed to emanate a noxious, sulfurous stench. His well-shaped arms seemed disproportionately long, and his hands sported dangerous, stiletto-like claws. His head was massive, split with wide flaring nostrils and large yellow cat-slit eyes that seemed to shine with their own light. On his head, two great horns like those of an eland spiraled slowly up to a height of about a meter above his skull. His shaggy mane seemed a striking contrast to his clean-shaven jaw and cheeks, while bright red pointed bat ears jutted from the sides of his head, standing erect and attentive like a Doberman pinscher's. His teeth were pointed, and two oversized, vicious canines added to the overall ghastliness of his countenance.

He smiled—not a fierce, diabolical smile, but a genuinely pleased and happy grin. "Well, well, well, what can I say but...welcome. Welcome to Hell."

He spread his arms out graciously.

"Satan?" One of the women whispered hoarsely.

"Ahriman? No, no, no. Nothing as notable as that. I am Xandern. One of the Yazatas. A minor functionary. I hope you are not too disappointed?" He seemed genuinely concerned.

One of the women shook her head and turned away sobbing.

"Well, let's see. What have we here today?" He picked up a red rectangle from his desk and began tapping on the device with the long sharp claw of his index finger.

"Hmm...hmm..." he repeated to himself as he gazed at the screen of his device, looking slightly puzzled.

"Lester Green?" he said, suddenly looking up at one of the men sitting in the uncomfortable metal chairs.

Rather than fear, this man seemed to radiate a quiet bold confidence—like someone used to sending back food at a restaurant after establishing some flaw in the meal that did not meet his exacting standards.

"There's been a mistake," he said softly, but with firm resolve. "I'm not supposed to be here."

"A mistake?" the demon said with a baffled look on his face. "Quite possibly, quite possibly. Things in Hell don't

always run as smoothly as one would like, do they?" He picked up the rectangle and after a few taps read aloud, "Let's see. Lester Green. 1294 Battle Lane. Forrest City, Arkansas. Wife: Sarah Green. Four children: Matthew, Mark, Jessie, and Caleb. Died while playing golf during a thunderstorm — struck by lightning," he mentioned as an aside to the other guests.

"Everything looks in order," the great demon said, with a little impatience in his voice.

"No, you see I was saved. Forever and for all time. I came forth at the preacher's call and was washed in the blood of the lamb. I'm saved by Christ. Who can snatch me from God's hand?"

As the man spoke he rose to his feet, drew his face upward, and threw his hands into the air crying, "Help me, Jesus!"

The Demon looked on quizzically. "You were a Christian then?"

"Yes. That's what I'm trying to tell you. I shouldn't be here. I've been saved," the man shouted, though with waning bravado.

"Well, there's your problem. You didn't join the one true religion."

"What? I'm telling you, I was a Christian. I read the Bible every day. I donated money to the TV evangelists every Sunday. And I was saved."

"No. Sorry. The true religion is Zoroastrianism, I'm afraid. Bit of bad luck there. Christianity certainly borrowed a great deal from the one true religion, but not enough, unfortunately. Not nearly enough."

"Zoor-what-ism? Never heard of it. How can that be the true religion?" The man looked confused.

"Zoroastrianism? Oh, there's never been but a few hundred thousand of them at any one time, mostly located in Iran and India, but that's it. The one true faith. If you're not a Zoroastrian, I'm afraid you are bound for Hell."

The man looked stunned and shocked. "It's not fair."

The demon gave a mirthful laugh. "Well, it was fair when you were sending all the Chinese to Hell who had never heard of Jesus. Wasn't it? And what a cruel and vicious Hell it was. And your Hell was not our short little correct-you-a-little Hell. This was eternal damnation. At least in the true Zoroastrianism system you eventually get out of Hell. Do you have any idea how long eternity is? My heavens, what an imagination you humans have. What kind of God would leave you burning forever? Most of you wouldn't do that to a neighbor's dog, even if it barked incessantly at two a.m. every morning. After about ten minutes watching a dog suffer in the kind of Hell you imagined God was going send his wicked children to, you would be pleading for the damned beast's mercy. It's crazy. Create a few beings; those that don't obey you roast forever? Give me a break." The demon shook his great head in wonder.

One of the women, a pretty girl with short red hair, raised her hand. "You mean we won't be in Hell forever?"

The Demon laughed. "Of course not. Of course not. Hell is for your edification and wisdom. Punishment? Yes. But not forever."

"So those people will get out?" the woman continued, pointing shakily to those in agony outside the window.

The demon considered for a moment. "I probably shouldn't tell you this . . . well, no harm's done, I've never really agreed with the policy anyway . . . but that's all just make-believe. We keep the office windows showing that scene just to get the new arrivals to take things seriously. Those are all actors. They get off in about a half hour. So . . . anyway, we'd better push on."

The humans seemed confused.

The demon rose to his feet. "Well, Lester the Christian, where shall we send you?"

"This isn't right," he screamed.

The demon was ignoring his tantrum. He began tapping his handheld device. "No . . . no, that's not it, no, no . . . maybe, no, ah! No, I shouldn't, but . . . no, that's too cruel . . . I really shouldn't."

Suddenly he gave a chuckle and sighed. "Oh, why not? The Great God created irony too."

Lester by this time was screaming at the top of his lungs about the injustice of it all.

"Injustice?" queried the demon sarcastically. "You were never concerned with justice a day in your life except when it was in your favor. Bye." With a tap of his claw to the rectangle the man disappeared briskly in mid-outrage, leaving the room in cold silence.

The demon was back on his device, humming a bit to himself. "That felt good. I hate those unthinking, unreflexive types. That Hell ought to humble him a bit . . . eternal Hell! What an imagination."

Everyone just stared at him as he busily tapped away.

"Julia Hanson?" He said looking at the same woman who had asked about the lake of fire outside the window. "Single. Professor of Biology at University of North Carolina at Chapel Hill. Confirmed atheist. Wrote a number of papers on the evolution of bumblebee society. Very interesting ones, too, I must say. Well, well, well, you must really be surprised to be here? Eh? Turns out there is a god after all. Now do you believe?"

The frightened woman could only shake her head and mutter, "I'm sure I've gone mad," but she did not seem convinced by her own words. After a moment she asked, "So there is a God?"

The demon nodded his head, "Yes, of course. The Wise Lord, Ahura Mazda. I'm his humble servant."

"I thought demons were under the control of Satan? Sort of the dark side of the Force."

"Why don't I ever get the people who have studied a little Zoroastrianism here?" he said, shaking his head sadly. "No, that's Christian. Ahriman has rebelled against God, but in charge of Hell? Heavens, no. How can you think God would let something like Hell exist if He's really in charge of the universe? Sheesh. Running a Hell is an art of such imagination and brilliance, how could anyone but the Wise God of Judgment be in charge?"

The woman looked down at her smock and mumbled, "I know more about bumble bees."

"Yes, you do," the demon said excitedly, tapping frantically as if he had just had a stroke of brilliance.

"There," he said smiling. "Bye."

She was gone.

A few more questions, a few more taps, some of the others begging, some silent, but one by one the people disappeared until one man remained sitting on his chair.

"Well, well, last the best of all the game, hey? . . . Soren Johansson, died of brain cancer . . . hmm, died young, only forty-five. Four children. Well, I'm sure they'll miss you. Looks like you were a good husband, good father . . . not a bad Mormon." He smiled. "You would have made a good Zoroastrian. Now, what Hell for you? Let's see, you liked to read . . . in fact it seems you loved books. Interesting."

Suddenly the demon looked up.

"Bye."

And so it began.

I FOUND THIS book around the $23^{439\text{th}}$ day of my stay in Hell. How odd to find a book that looks as if I wrote it, when it's really just one of the random possibilities that exist here. It was close enough to the actual events that I will place it in the slot to see if it changes my fate. The slight variations are trivial and of no consequence. How does one begin to describe infinities of eons? How can such a small word as "eon" describe a length of time that is more akin to eternity than any measurable time span? There is no metaphor I can use to give you a sense of the time that's passed here. My earth life was so long ago that by now trillions of universes like the one in which I lived on earth have come and gone. Countless such must have blown into existence in innumerable big bangs, each with a billion generations of suns flaring into existence, then burning out into a fine, dull brown dust. After this long I am not bitter—I barely feel at all. Now I only search.

1

THE BEGINNING

UPON LEAVING THE DEMON, I WAS DISORIENTED AND COULD only tell I was in an immense, spacious building. Strangely, to my surprise and despite my terror, confusion, and fear, I felt better than I had for years. Before my death I had suffered terribly, but I noticed quickly I was now in perfect health. I stared at my hands. My wedding ring was gone. The scars and age spots had disappeared, leaving only the scattered freckles from my sunny youth. I touched my front teeth, surprised that those lost so long ago in a head-on collision with a drunk driver had been replaced and the once jagged row of my staggering bottom teeth was straight. I suppose I was also surprised I had a body at all. As a Mormon I believed I would eventually get a perfect body after the resurrection, but immediately after death I was supposed to go to a spirit world. It was clear this was not what had happened.

Feeling lost and confused, I was overwhelmed with a desire to pray, as I had so often during my mortal earth life. While alive, I often knelt in prayer and asked for blessings and sought direction from the Lord. As then, I dropped to my knees and began to pray, but I was overwhelmed with doubt and fear. Could I pray in Hell? Could I pray my way out of Hell? Who was I praying to now? The God I believed in was a kind, wise Heavenly Father who loved me and sent His son to redeem me. He had an eternal plan, which would end in my deification if I lived according to the commandments and obtained the proper ordinances here in this life. I was supposed to go to a spirit world to share the gospel with other dead spirits until the resurrection. I would then go to the Celestial Kingdom and live with my wife forever — becoming a God like my Heavenly Father and continuing His work of redeeming the uncreated intelligences that filled the universe. This Hell did not fit anywhere in my belief system.

I began to cry. I bawled like a baby — tears falling onto the white smock. I prayed, but all the while I was shrouded in blind confusion. I knew nothing about Zoroastrianism. I missed my wife and children. I missed the familiar trappings of my home, my work, and my routines. Questions plagued me. Was I supposed to pray? The demon said God was called Ahura Mazda. Was he kind and loving? What was his nature? Was it even a he, like the God I'd worshiped all my life as a Mormon? Could it be a Goddess? I had no way to know. How do you pray if you don't know what God is like?

Maybe God was a demon — that would explain much of the misery of earth life. Would prayer do any good? I could not tell.

Suddenly, no more than a few minutes after I had arrived, or so it felt to me, the lights went out, and in the dark I wept until I slept.

At six a.m. — and I knew it was six o'clock because there was a large (almost two meters in diameter) round clock near me on the wall, like a giant version of the kind that hung above my elementary school teacher's desk, and underneath it was a digital readout that said, "Year 0000000, Day 2" — the lights came on as quickly as they had gone out the night before. I surveyed my surroundings carefully for the first time. I was in a long corridor about twelve feet wide. Running along one side of the hall was a thick metal pipe–like railing about four feet high, intended, no doubt, to keep me from falling into a fearsome chasm. The railing was painted a soft brownish red and fashioned with rounded corners and turns like the low fences that front the wire cages at the zoo. It extended down the endless hall until it disappeared in a vanishing point, almost as if I were looking into parallel facing mirrors that give the illusion they go on and on forever. Looking across the railing to the other side of the chasm, which seemed as bottomless as the corridor seemed long, I could see I was on an upper floor of a vast building. The floors on the other side of the chasm looked like a series of matching floors to the one on which I stood. The floors across the hundred-foot span extended upward and downward as far as the eye could see. On every floor were rows upon rows of books. Millions of them (you will see soon what a terrible underestimate this is). It struck me as nothing so much as a prison block with books arranged on shelves on each floor rather than jail cells.

The floor was carpeted with the drab, gray, highly functional carpet that seems ubiquitous in public buildings. People were scattered everywhere on both sides of the abyss, some standing, staring blankly, others walking in a daze, some weeping uncontrollably, some kneeling in desperate prayer as I had done last night. Everyone looked as stunned and frightened as I felt. No one looked interested in talking, and everyone seemed as preoccupied as I was with trying to understand this strange afterlife into which we had unexpectedly been tossed.

I turned back to investigate my surroundings. In the vicinity of where I slept, I found a break in the shelves of books. Looking over the rail to the other side, where I had a panoramic view of this strange building, I could see that such breaks in the rows of books occurred about every three hundred yards or so on each floor. The breaks were identical: on each one there was a round clock with large black hands and a digital date readout in the center of the clock-face. In front of every clock in the hallway was a small kiosk near the railing. Next to the clock was a sign with a set of rules and advice. There was also an open entrance into a small room. I peered into the closest and found it led to a small chamber furnished with seven neatly made beds, the frame being constructed of the same metal that fashioned the railing. On each bed was a mattress, fitted sheets, pillow, a blanket, and a smock identical to the one I was wearing. There was also a drinking fountain near the entrance. Attached to the little bedroom was a spacious bathroom with a shower, sink, and a generous full-length mirror on the wall opposite the sink. There were no necessities like toothbrushes or razors of any kind; however, there was toilet paper, tissue, and soap in a pump bottle. Somehow I had always assumed going to the bathroom was something of such an earthly nature that it would be unnecessary in the afterlife. There were to be many surprises.

I looked in the mirror and discovered not the gaunt, forty-five-year-old dying-of-cancer me that stared back from the glass the last time I looked at my reflection, but a fit version of my twenty-five-year-old self. My body was sleek and well muscled, with my hair neatly cut and parted down the middle as I'd always worn it. My teeth were white and straighter than I'd imagined was possible. For a brief second I had a light-hearted feeling of satisfaction. I *had* been resurrected, as I'd always believed in my religion. I flexed my muscles and stood admiring my flawless grin, greatly pleased by how healthy I felt. Thinking that my resurrected body would be indestructible, as my Mormon beliefs held, I tried to scratch myself. I was disappointed that without difficulty I drew blood. And it hurt. This was not the type of afterlife I had always envisioned. Not by a long shot.

A man came into the bathroom and saw me preening before my newly fit reflection. He turned around with a quick "Sorry!" and left me alone to my marveling.

I went back to the corridor to look at the sign placed next to the clock. The letters were large and black, printed on a reflective background—like the surface of a speed-limit sign. This is what it said:

> Welcome to Hell. This Hell is based upon a short story by Jorge Luis Borges from your world called "The Library of Babel." Here you will find all the books that can possibly be written. When you are ready to leave, find the book describing your earthly life story (without errors, e.g., in spelling, grammar, etc.) and submit the story through the slot below this sign. If the story is accepted, you will be admitted into a glorious heaven filled with wonders and joys beyond your imagination. During your stay you may be interested in reading a book on Zoroastrianism. By special arrangement, there is one on every floor. The other books are randomized. The food kiosk will provide whatever you would like to eat. Just ask for it. We would ask that you please follow a few simple rules during your stay in Hell:
>
> 1. Please be kind. Treat others as you would like to be treated. Failure to do this will bring unhappiness and misery to you and your fellow citizens.
>
> 2. Do not get discouraged. Remember nothing lasts forever. Someday this will be a distant memory.

3. Please leave towels on the floor if you wish them to be cleaned. Hang up those you wish to use again.

4. Books not in your possession will be returned to their original place on the stacks every night. A book will be considered in your possession if you are touching it.

5. If you are killed you will be restored to life on the following day. Please try to avoid death as much as possible.

6. All contracts, bonds, commitments, covenants, pledges, and promises entered into prior to your entering Hell are null and void. This includes, but is not limited to: debt, marriage, natural births and adoptions, requirements of citizenship, military obligations, student loans, etc.

7. Remember you are never really alone. Although it may feel like it for very long stretches of time.

8. Please don't write on, mark, or mar library materials. Although repairs are made nightly, we would like to keep repairs to a minimum.

9. Lastly, you are here to learn something. Don't try to figure out what it is. This can be frustrating and unproductive.

We hope you enjoy your stay here. We have done all we can to make your stay a pleasant and instructive one.

I stared at the rules a long time. Especially number six. As a Mormon, I had always believed I was married for eternity, but now my wife was gone? Was she here somewhere? Were my children missing me? Was everyone here who had ever lived? No. I remembered the demon tapping away on his handheld device, seemingly to send people to a variety of Hells.

Still, all I had believed in during my life appeared to be mistaken. Gone just like that. All my hopes. All my prayers. It was all wrong. I remembered what little I had read about Zoroastrianism: Iranian, started in approximately 600 BC. I found I could recall every detail of my life; every event ever experienced I could remember with perfect clarity. I could remember every word on every page I'd ever read. Every conversation. Every tax form I'd ever filled out. I could reconstruct every second of every day I'd been alive from the moment of my birth until the day I finally shut my eyes at the end.

This clarity of memory surprised me the first time I tried reviewing the past, but it was all there. (This was to be the greatest curse of Hell. Sometimes I would replay my entire life again and again for thousands of years. Remembering all the things I could have done differently, all the things . . . no. I won't go there now. I must tell this story.)

The first few days were ones of discovery. Everyone just sort of nodded to one another; I think we were all disoriented and confused. It was not until about two p.m. on the second day that I noticed I felt hungry. I had seen someone using the food kiosk earlier. The man had just walked up and said, "Roast beef sandwich," and one appeared on the tray before him. I decided to be more specific. "A roast beef sandwich, with provolone cheese, Dijon mustard, lettuce, tomato, and mayonnaise on rye bread." Much to my surprise, exactly what I asked for appeared. "Could I get a diet Coke, too?" It appeared likewise and looked and tasted like a diet Coke. "And how about a vanilla shake?" As an afterthought I added, "Like the kind at the Purple Aardvark on Second South in Mountain Grove, Utah." It came. Just like I remembered it. The taste, texture, and presentation — including being served upside down in a bowl — it was all the same. There were no tables, so I sat on the floor under the railing, dangling my feet over the edge and staring at the rows and rows of floors on the other side of the abyss. Across the chasm, people were also reading the rules, wandering around, and, just as we were, starting small conversations. Some were using the kiosk and eating.

"Mind if I join you?" The speaker was a young man — but then so was I. That thought cheered me. He was wearing the same cotton robe we all wore, thick with wide sleeves that fell to about the forearm, with a hole cut out at the top wide enough to expose the bottom of our necks. It hung loosely and modestly to about mid-calf. Our feet were bare. The temperature seemed pleasant — not too cold or too hot.

I motioned to the floor and he plopped down beside me. We dangled our legs over the edge, our arms resting on the railing. He was eating an apple and had a can of V8 Juice.

"Strange Hell," he said, motioning to the people on the other side of the chasm.

"Not what I expected," I agreed.

"Not Zoroastrian either then?"

"Mormon."

"Ah. I was agnostic, so of course I wasn't thinking of this as the final ending," he said, waving his arm around randomly. "You from Utah?"

"Yeah. You?"

"I'm from Santa Rosa, California."

"Never been there."

We sat silently for a few minutes, eating our lunches thoughtfully. I think at the time we were still taking it all in. He drained his can and tossed it down into the bottomless space separating us from the floors on the other side. We both watched it fall until it grew so small it disappeared. We both held our breath waiting for some sound of it hitting the bottom. It never came.

"Deep hole," he said conversationally.

"I wonder how far down to the bottom?" I said, inclining my head downward.

He shrugged, shaking his.

"I can't imagine. What did you think of the rules?" he asked, taking another bite of his apple.

"Not very informative. Seemed simple enough. I wonder what happens if you don't follow them? I mean it says if we aren't kind to each other we'll have a miserable time of it. Is that because we're punished in some way?"

The man looked at me, somewhat frightened. He finally asked if I'd seen the lake of fire and brimstone. I told him what our demon had said about them all being actors.

"What a strange place. Well, I can tell you one thing. I'm getting out of here as soon as possible. I'm going to find my book and get it in that slot in two shakes of a lamb's tail," he said determinedly. "I'm not going to stay in this place for twenty years before starting and then spend another twenty looking for it."

I nodded and said I would be doing the same. Spending twenty years looking for a book did not sound pleasant. What if it stretched to fifty or even a hundred years? I wondered. Looking around at the size of this library it would not be hard to imagine that there were more than a million books lining the shelves that stretched up, down, and side to side as far as the eye could see.

We talked most of the afternoon. I told him about my death. He told me about his. He died of a heart attack at age ninety-three in his sleep. It sounded like a pleasant way to die.

"Of course, I was a little surprised to find myself sitting in a room with a demon and watching a scene from Dante's *Inferno*. I'm still a little surprised to find myself here. But it's all so real. There's a sense of actuality that I just can't dismiss. I'm fairly pleased to find myself so young and strong again. If only Sally could see me now. Wouldn't she get a kick out of this? My, what a strange universe we live in."

About this time we noticed a young lady standing by the kiosk next to us who seemed to be waiting for a chance to ask us something.

"Hello," my companion said simply. She looked sad and lost. And seemed near enough to tears not to be able to hold them back much longer.

"Are we in Hell?" She shuddered.

We both stood up awkwardly. I looked at my companion and he looked at me. He spoke first.

"We think so."

With that, she let go and sobbed bitterly into her hands. I looked at my companion, and tears were running down his face. It took me a minute to realize I was crying too. She looked up and soon we found ourselves in a group hug bawling furiously.

We looked at one another, all strangers, all lost and alone, and the absurdity of our situation struck us. We all suddenly burst into an awkward laughter that just as quickly melted into sobs again.

It took some time, but we eventually gathered a measure of composure. I ran into the nearby bathroom and grabbed some toilet paper and passed it around to our small troop. We introduced ourselves. I learned my companion's name was Elliott Callington. The woman was named Larisa Sims. She had died of breast cancer at age fifty-four. It seemed odd, standing there in Hell, but understanding how we each had died seemed the most important thing about us. I see now, however, that it was only because it was the freshest thing on our minds — and something we had worried about all our lives in one way or another. Now it was over. We were dead. And now we were in Hell.

We three talked until the lights went out again. The

only light visible was a faint greenish glow coming out of the room with the beds. The source of the light turned out to be a dimly lit exit sign facing into the room. Inside, the room was dark, but each of us felt or maneuvered our way to one of the beds. Last time I'd looked at the clock it was about 9:45, so I supposed it was about 10:00 when the lights went out. I lay there a while, but could not sleep. How strange it all was. I decided to try to see if I could get a glass of warm milk to help me sleep. I felt my way to the kiosk and said, "Warm milk, please," but nothing happened. I tried a couple of times, but apparently the machines only worked when the lights were on.

As I made my way back to the bed, Larisa asked if I had tried the kiosk just now. I replied in the affirmative, explained my failure to get some milk, and then climbed into bed. Other than the breathing of my companions, I was stunned by the stillness. I'd spent the last month in a hospital and was used to commotion, ticks, hums, beeps, and the hush-swish of air-conditioning systems going on and off, nurses coming in and out at all times of night. Here in Hell it was absolutely still. Not even the whisper of any air movement. The stillness of the grave? I shuddered and curled up into my blanket. The mattress was firm and comfortable, and I soon drifted into a deep, dreamless sleep.

I AWOKE WHEN the light came on. Elliott was first to the bathroom, and I could hear the shower running. Larisa was still asleep. I drank from the drinking fountain and walked outside and asked for a glass of cold orange juice. I leaned over the railing and drank my juice, looking deep into the crevasse between the floors bracketing our side and the other opposite. I don't think I'd ever seen anything so deep. Not even the Grand Canyon had seemed so vast. After a few minutes, Larisa joined me in staring over the side.

"I used to be afraid of heights. But this looks even beyond my fear. It looks like it goes on forever," she remarked.

"Maybe it does." (I was wrong of course. It does end. There is a bottom. But "forever" would have been a better word. "Forever and ever" would hardly have described it. "Infinity" is even too small a word to describe the vastness of the distance to the bottom. But I've stood upon the bottom floor. The human mind cannot comprehend what it took to reach, but I've been there.)

For the first time since our arrival, Larissa and I walked over to the shelves of books and pulled one down. Each volume appeared to be identical on the outside. They were bound in light brown high-quality calfskin. The edges were gilded in bright gold, and the paper was a thick heavy bond — substantial and bright white, fibrous, and nicely stitched into the binding. Each page was a solid block of text. An ordinary book by all appearances — except the text was complete gibberish. A random splash of capital and lowercase characters, punctuation marks, and other characters like &, *, $,

and #. Here is a line from the first page of the first book
I picked up:

Aj;kLJjppOjnfe7ImNB2uyS@;jHnMBVFghT/.hk
%hKh'2jh<,bYblZl@)m$'n@gDE#zB/,,JhqWXvd 7

Every page had a similar look.

"These books are nothing but garbage," Larisa said
in a disgusted voice. "When I was looking at these, I was
thinking about a lifetime spent reading great works of
literature. Now I get it — this is Hell; an eternity surrounded by books, but they're all nonsense." She gave a
sarcastic laugh and heaved the book over the railing.

A man wandered over to us. "I see you've discovered
the quality of our library."

"I can't believe it," I said, picking up another volume
and staring at the textual salad of symbols.

"My name is Bob, but my friends all called me
Biscuit."

"How do you do ... Biscuit?"

I continued to pull books off the shelf and flip
through them. I was having a hard time believing all of
the books were just collections of random characters.

The man calling himself Biscuit seemed mildly
amused. I was pulling them off the shelf, paging rapidly
through them and then, like Larisa, tossing them over
the side. More people joined us, and soon a fair number
of us were looking through books and tossing them over
the side, most of them making the same sorts of com-
ments.

"I can't believe it. Such nice books, and every one of them filled with nonsense."

"This isn't right! Is it?"

"This is Hell. This really is Hell."

One woman was laughing hysterically and just tossing books over the side. She wasn't even looking at them.

I have to admit I found a certain strange pleasure in heaving books over the side. It was a feeling akin to popping bubble-wrap. Taking a book of nonsense, tossing it over the rail, and watching it until it disappeared flapping wildly into the oblivion below gave me a strange satisfaction, a small sense of purpose. Only Biscuit refrained from helping the general effort to clean the shelves. He just sat there smiling, shaking his head.

"I see," he said to no one in particular. "We really are in the Library of Babel."

A woman standing next to me, watching our books fall like a pair of wounded ducks spiraling to the ground, inquired politely, "The Library of Babel?"

"This is the Library of Babel," he shouted. "We're in it. Not like Borges described it, but this is it, the same idea."

Several people turned their attention to Biscuit, including me.

"What's the library of Babel?" another man asked, repeating the woman's question.

"Don't you see?" Biscuit was fairly animated, and most of the people who had been launching books into the chasm had turned to listen to him.

"It's written on the sign with the rules outside the rest areas. It says this Hell is based on a story by Borges. I remember the story. Look, the books all end on page four hundred ten, just like the books in his story. And look at this. They're all in blocks of" — here he started counting — "yes, forty lines, and I'll bet there are" — he started counting again — "yes. Eighty characters per line, just as Borges described. Amazing. We're in the Library of Babel."

Someone asked a third time, a little more impatiently than the first two inquiries, "What's the Library of Babel?" Biscuit looked around him and saw that an audience of about fifty people now gave him its undivided attention.

"Well," he began in a lecturesome tone, "imagine a library that contains not just every book that has been written, but every book that could be written. I remember the story exactly. How strange. But the basic idea from Borges's story is that the library contains every possible book. So somewhere in here is a book of all *A's*, a book of all periods, or a book of semicolons, or *B's*. Any letter. There's a book that alternates *A's* and *B's* for its entire length, but most books are just a random collection of symbols."

"So there's a book that's half *A's* and in the second half all *B's*," proposed one woman.

"Yes. But more than that, every book ever written is there. And every book ever written is there backwards."

One man raised his hand like a student in a classroom, and Biscuit acknowledged him.

"It can't have every book," the man said, tilting his head and looking ridiculous as he affected a knowing and wise demeanor. "Some books are longer than four hundred ten pages. Take *War and Peace*, for example."

He looked around, nodding his head trying to find someone to acknowledge his point.

"No. Don't you see?" Biscuit said. "*War and Peace* would be in multiple volumes."

"With blank pages after it ended, completing the last volume," added the woman standing next to me.

"Or with the life story of Leo Tolstoy at the end," added another woman.

"Both," said Biscuit. "There's even one with the history of Leo Tolstoy's nose hair completing the volume. But most are going to be pure and utter nonsense—random characters, with no order. Mostly nonsense."

"So there's a version of *War and Peace* with the main character named Fred instead of Pierre," said a man to no one in particular.

"And another where Mark Twain and Huck Finn join the war against Napoleon," added another woman.

"But mostly nonsense," Biscuit added again softly.

Everyone was silent a moment.

"That's what the sign out front means," the speaker was my new friend Elliott. "We have to find our own life story to get out of here."

"In one or two volumes," asked a man in despair, "or ten or twelve?"

Biscuit continued almost to himself, "There's a second-by-second account of our lives, probably in multiple volumes, a minute-by-minute account, an hour-by-hour, a day-by-day. There's one that covers the events of our lives as viewed by our mothers, one by our fathers, one by our neighbors, one by our dogs. There must be thousands of our biographies here. Which one do they want, I wonder?"

Everyone seemed stunned, thinking about the different volumes in the library.

"You mean there's a biography of everything and everyone in this library. There's even a biography of the guppies in my fish tank?"

"Yes. Anything that can be written is there. The history of your big toe as viewed from the perspective of your shoe is there. Anything you can imagine, anything you can picture being written is here is this library." Biscuit seemed to be astonishing even himself.

"It must have billions and billions of books," one woman said. "If there's a biography for anyone who's ever lived, and every guppy that ever lived, and every worm that ever lived, there must be billions and billions of books."

"Wouldn't it be infinite?" said another man shakily.

"I'm not sure. I don't think so," Biscuit said slowly. "If we have four hundred and ten pages, forty lines of eighty characters, and a finite number of characters, there's a finite number of books I would think. But it's large. Very large."

We were all silent at the thought of the task before us. In this library of mostly meaningless books there was a book that described our life story. We had to find that one book. It could take millions of years, I thought. (Millions of years. Ha!)

Most of the people had lost interest in opening the books and had begun conversations in small groups. I fell in with Biscuit and a woman named Dolores. Biscuit had lived most of his life as a homeless schizophrenic. He earned the name Biscuit when he refused to give up two dinner rolls to a couple of policeman arresting him. He told them, "These are the brain and heart of the world. Were I to give them up, the world would die and waste away." He spent his life believing the world was dying, because one of his cellmates had eaten them while he was asleep.

Dolores had been a housewife married to a factory worker in Detroit. She raised four children and then opened a ceramics shop after they had grown and left home. Her life had been rich and happy. She died at her daughter's house surrounded by those she loved.

In both stories of my companions, their young looks contrasted with their sagacity and age. I had died young and never really felt I had matured. I remember my own father, a real man of the house, someone who knew what it was to be a man. He radiated confidence. I never felt like that. I felt as if I were an imposter all the time I was raising my kids. I felt lost and helpless. I was flying by the seat of my pants, always with a feeling I was not doing things right. Compared to my own father, I seemed completely clueless. My dad was still living when I died. I hope he ends up in a nice Hell.

A nice Hell. I laughed at the thought. This wasn't a

bad place. It seemed like a tedious Hell, but there was plenty to eat, good company, and it sounded like after a while we would eventually get out.

We three went off to a nearby kiosk. I found Elliott and Larisa there and introduced everyone.

"I guess we've got our work cut out for us," Elliott observed positively. "It's too bad we're starting the search in the middle. Maybe we should find where the library ends. You know, start at the beginning."

"It's not a bad idea," Biscuit said, "at least we wouldn't accidently redo a floor or something."

Larisa smiled. "I'm still not convinced there's not an infinity of books. How can there be a limit to the number of books that can be written?"

Dolores and Elliott nodded in agreement. (I'll have to admit I was a little skeptical myself, but as you'll see, I eventually met someone who had calculated the number of books in the library. There *is* a finite number.)

The clock was moving toward ten p.m., and I thought the lights would probably go out soon. I went over and ordered warm milk, and it appeared, piping hot, the way I like it. I chose the same bedroom and the same bed I had slept in the night before. My two friends did the same. No one else came in with us, and we had the room to ourselves. What creatures of habit we are. After only a few nights in Hell we had settled into a comfortable routine. As I drank my milk, the lights went out and that utter stillness returned. My thoughts were restless now, and I was in no mood for sleep. How far was it to the end of the hallway in which we lived? Was it further than a mile? What if it were a hundred miles? How many books would that be? What if it were a thousand? It wasn't that far, surely.

2

THE FIRST WEEK IN HELL

As ALWAYS, THE BOOKS WE THREW OVER THE RAIL INTO THE great chasm between the two great bookcases were restored to their proper place on the shelves the next morning. Every morning we leafed through more books in hopes of finding our story and then, after noting the consistent sea of random text, tirelessly heaved them over the side. It was getting discouraging. I had not found even a single sentence that made sense.

However, a few days later, Biscuit started dancing and shouting with joy. He called us over and we all looked in envy when he showed us he had found something that made sense. It was the phrase "sack it."

"What does it mean?" Sam asked. (Sam was a short, quiet young man, who had formed a sort of clique with Elliott, Larisa, Biscuit, Dolores, and me.)

Biscuit looked thoughtful. "I'm not sure. Let's see, a sack is something you use to carry something in. Maybe it means I'm going to go somewhere soon and will need a sack."

"What makes you think it means anything . . ." I started to say, but I looked at Biscuit and he had begun to cry, then sob. Tears slid down his cheeks, and he smiled at us, nodding his head as if affirming something we could not understand. We all were a little surprised. Dolores softly put her arm around him, and he turned to hug her as he continued to weep.

"I'm sorry," he said through his tears, "it's just that . . ." He broke off, then said, "When I was alive, I . . ." Finally, after another bout of weeping, he steadied himself, laughed at himself, and started again. "When I was alive on earth, as you know, I was homeless and chronically mentally ill. I had an old green army laundry bag that I carried everything in. It was a sack that held everything I owned. A couple of times at night I've woken up reaching for it like I used to. It was my most prized possession. I carried that sack for twenty-three years, until one day the bottom fell out. I couldn't let it go even then. I hitchhiked to the Vietnam memorial and placed it on the monument right above a friend's name."

There was a moment of silence as we considered this.

"You were in Nam?" Elliott asked. Biscuit just nodded.

"I was in the South Pacific in WWII. If you ask me that was more of a Hell than this giant bookshelf."

Dolores began telling a rather silly story of how a sack was significant in her life when she had carried one from an exclusive department store with her to school and one of the cool girls had been jealous and she and her friends had laughingly ripped it to smithereens.

Within a few minutes we all found meaningful, or terrible, stories about sacks in our lives. I even shared a story about a sack I threw away at Christmastime with a fifty-dollar check in it.

Biscuit, though, took it as a sign that all would be well. And Dolores as a sign of comfort and hope.

To be honest, I thought it was just a random word, but I didn't say anything to the others. They seemed particularly moved by Biscuit's story. He held on to the book all that day and took it to bed with him that night. Sure enough, because he'd held on to it, the book wasn't returned to its place on the shelf in the morning. It was still in his arms when he woke up. All the rest of the week he carried it with him, much like the sack he once loved so much. After two days, he found even more meaning in the word. It turned out that "sack" was on page 345, on line 21. Which if you reverse the 21 makes 1 2 3 4 5 backward — sort of. The word "sack" was found starting on letter 27 of the line and ending on letter 30. Which are both divisible by 3, which if you multiply by the 2 and the 7 in 27 respectively, gives you 6 and 21. Now, since you still need to get a single digit, you divide the 21 by 3, which gives you 7 back, so now not only do you have 1 2 3 4 5, you have 6 and 7. Now go back to the 27 and divide by 3, so you get 9, and divide the 30 by 3, and you get what? 10. So then you have 1 2 3 4 5 6 7 9 10.

"Now," says Biscuit, "take the three and the zero in thirty and add them together, and you get three, which added to the last number in the first chain you found, which is five, gives you eight. So the numbers of the page, line, and character produce the numbers one, two, three, four, five, six, seven, eight, nine, and ten."

Biscuit was beside himself. His first few days in Hell were ringing with meaning.

"What does that mean?" I asked innocently enough, unsure of what finding the first ten cardinal numbers in such a convoluted fashion meant.

Biscuit looked at me like a schoolmaster looks at an errant rapscallion.

"Don't you see? This gives us the number of years we'll search before finding what we seek. Sack signifies that the thing that has the most meaning to us here, the book with our life story, will be found in ten years. It gives the times and seasons of our stay here. It might mean ten days or ten weeks, but I suspect given the magnitude of our task ten years is not unreasonable."

"Oh," I said.

Dolores was not too happy with his interpretation. "Ten years? That's a long time to stay in a library. I hope it's days or weeks. My heavens, ten years. Here. We'll all go batty."

THAT NIGHT IN the absolute silence and darkness I lay on my lonely bed thinking. Thinking about the length of the library. I liked the idea of finding the end of a floor — if just to confirm there was an end to these rows and rows of books. Then we could look for the bottom, or the top, and start a systematic search for our book. I made up my mind. After a week of being in this place, I also wanted to see how many people were here. I thought it strange we'd only found other white people, that all of us spoke English, and that all of us made reference only to things we all understood. As far as we had been able to gather from the group around our area, we had all died within sixty years of each other. I was curious if this held throughout the library.

I suppose what I really wondered was whether my wife was hidden somewhere in the vast reaches of this building. Maybe she had lived out her life and died and come to this same strange place. Maybe I could find her.

At some point I must have fallen asleep, because suddenly I found the lights coming back on, and the brightness of morning revealing our world and pushing back the abyss of darkness that made up our nights.

Our little gang of five typically gathered at the kiosk in the morning, where the others would have a cup of coffee. I took my first cup ever on this morning. Being a Mormon, I had never even tasted coffee, let alone drunk a whole cupful. How could that matter now? Zoroastrianism had been shown true, and I was in a Hell that had no prohibitions against it. Still, it was hard. Lifelong habits are not easily broken. Keeping the Word of Wisdom, as we Mormons called our health code, had always been taken as a sign of my righteousness, my worthiness to attend the holy temple, and to participate fully in the church. Even here in Hell, after a lifetime of keeping the Word of

Wisdom, I was having an ugly time deciding whether to try a cup.

"This is my first cup of coffee," I announced somewhat apprehensively to the usual gang. "Any suggestions?"

It started a small argument when Biscuit suggested black so I could experience the taste in its full and unadulterated purity. Larisa insisted I ease into it. "Don't you remember how nasty it was the first time you tasted it? Let's not scare him away for heaven's sake."

Larisa prevailed, and I ordered a mild mocha. Everyone watched, holding their breaths as I brought the small white cup to my lips and took a sip of the rich brown liquid. It tasted like crap. The most bitter and disappointed taste I had ever encountered. Everyone laughed and patted me on the back. They all congratulated the Mormon boy for breaking with his past.

I finished the cup, but I felt like I had betrayed something deep within me. Only a little over a week in Hell and I had abandoned a lifelong belief. What if this was just some sort of trial God had arranged to test my backbone? What if this Hell was really all a ruse concocted by God to see what I was made of? But no, there was something real and final about this Hell. I can't describe it, but there was a deep sense that this was more real than anything I had experienced on earth. The difference in the quality of consciousness between dreaming and being awake was close to the difference between our old earth life and the one there. This reality carried with it a profound sense of itself — a deep sense that this Hell was indeed just what it seemed to be. There was a truth in it that denied second-guessing. I really felt and now believed Zoroastrianism was the one true religion and I was truly and undeniably in Hell, and would be here until I found a way out. Also — and this seemed odd to me — just as I believed in the physical reality presented to me, I believed I would find the book about my life I was expected to find and one day slip it into the appointed slot and be free. I wondered why I believed it all. But I clearly did.

Even when I tried to formulate doubts about my experience, I found I was only playing with doubting. I really believed I was where the demon said I was. I was in Hell and there was no denying it. It was as if my entire consciousness, like a computer program, now had a script imposed on it compelling me to believe this experience was an actuality that brooked no argument. It was as if my neural wiring had been rewritten in accordance with a modified version of Descartes's famous dictum, "I think therefore I am." Now it was "I think I am in Hell, therefore I am."

Despite this perception of reality, I felt strangely myself as well. I was still the Mormon, still the geologist, still as curious; I still loved my wife and missed my children terribly. I thought about them all the time and wondered what they were doing right then. I wondered if "right then" even made sense. Did time in Hell work the same as time on earth? Did my week there take a week on earth? Did it take a thousand years? Or twenty nanoseconds? Was there no frame of reference? Of course not, I thought, there are people here who died over fifty years ago, and I'd met a woman who died thirty years after me. Yet here the days passed as I remembered them. Time on the large clock seemed to sweep through a second the same way it did on clocks back on earth.

While I was thinking about this, Biscuit tried to get some cigarettes. They did not come. He then tried a shot of whiskey, which, to his delight, appeared in a shot glass in the kiosk. He tossed it down with a bright eye and asked for another.

"It's the real thing," he declared as he knocked back the second. He asked for a third and it came. Strangely, after six or seven there still seemed to be no effect on him. After twenty, he was getting frustrated.

"It's all fake," he declared. Suddenly his eyes lost their focus, and he staggered against the rail.

"He's plastered," Dolores giggled.

"Um not plasssserd," he slurred. "One more for the rood," he coaxed the kiosk, and it gave him one. "Hell, gife mme a boodle."

The kiosk gave him a bottle, and he opened it and started chugging.

It wasn't long before others joined in the fun. Even people across the gulf saw what was going on over on our side and started rounds of drinks.

This was too much for me. Drinking? I was still reeling from ordering an "evil" cup of coffee. So as everyone began drinking, I walked away. For the last week or so I had not ventured much further than a couple hundred yards or so from the bedroom near where I had appeared. But now I just wanted to get away. People were carrying large steins of beer and telling me to drink up. It was Hellfest. I could not. So I started to run down the hall. Always a good runner when I was young, I found my new youthful body was in wonderful shape. I would guess I was doing about a six-and-a-half-minute mile and felt like I could do it forever.

So I ran. I ran for a little over three hours. (The strange thing in Hell is, you always know what time it is. The great clocks are always visible.) Along the way, I met others like myself, but, strangely, they were all white and all spoke English with an American accent as they waved or gave a short greeting. After a brief rest and a little orange juice I started again. I was determined to answer the question of how large the library was by finding the end of the floor I was on. It could not be too far. Maybe a hundred miles or so. If I ran, say, eight miles in an hour that would put me at about sixty-four miles a day.

So on I ran. I ran past people I did not know, past the endless stacks of books, bedrooms, and kiosks. By about six p.m. I was starting to tire and stopped to rest. The people gathered around as I came to a sweaty stop near where they were gathered talking quietly. I introduced myself and told them what I was doing. They seemed excited about the project and told me I could stay in their bedroom. I was a little disturbed that they thought it was "theirs," because I recognized that in searching for our books we were going to have to move around. I slipped away to take a quick shower and took one of the robes lying on one of the beds. I paused for a moment, hoping I had not offended anyone by co-opting their space.

I knew, however, that sometime during the day, at some point when everyone had left the bedrooms, all the beds would be made, bathrooms cleaned, and a clean robe laid on the bed with a new pair of slippers. Any dirty towels on the floors would be replaced and all would be tidied up. But being new to this area of the library it was impossible for me to tell if any of the beds had been claimed, so I just grabbed one.

I walked back out and held what I would learn to call the usual conversation. Who I was. Where I had lived my life. What wonderful things I had accomplished. The things that had been left undone. Who I missed and what I should have done differently and, finally, how I died.

At about 9:50 p.m., I went into the bedroom and asked where I should sleep. In this room, it turned out only two of the bunks were claimed. I was so tired from the run that I curled up and went to sleep. As soon as the lights were on in the morning, I was running again.

On and on, from one day to another, I ran. I started counting my paces and timing myself, and just as I'd guessed, I was doing a little under seven minutes a mile —not a record pace, but fast enough. A week went by and there seemed to be no end to this corridor. Sometimes I leaned far out over the rail and looked to the vanishing point to see if I could get a hint of the end of the corridor. Sometimes I thought I could see it, but it never appeared, and really I could not see anything but a vanishing point far in the distance. Straight on the shelves ran until they disappeared into a tiny point that never changed, never gave a hint that I was approaching an end. For three weeks I ran, covering I estimate about fourteen hundred miles, and nothing ever changed.

I began to think how strange it seemed that I never met a single person of color. Not an Asian, not a black person, not a Hispanic, not anything but a sea of white American Caucasians. Was there no diversity in Hell? What did this endless repetition of sameness and of uniformity in people and surroundings mean?

In the third week I quit. I felt like this was purposeless. There seemed to be no end. What if there wasn't an end? What if Dolores was right? What if there was an infinite number of books, what if there really was no end? Suddenly, I missed my new friends. I had only known them a little over a week, but I'd formed a bond with them and, out here, I had not met anyone else I'd become so attached to. I wanted to see them and talk to them. I wanted to hear Biscuit talk about his sack. I wanted to listen to Larisa laugh.

I ran back. It took me almost as long, but I ran with a new intensity. I wanted to find my friends again. I hardly said anything to anyone on the way back. All I could think about was finding a face I knew.

And suddenly there they were. And sober, too. (I'd entertained a fear they would still be sloshing drunk.) What a reunion. They had wondered desperately what had happened to me. No one could much remember the day through the fog of the alcohol. When I left, some wondered if I had gotten drunk and thrown myself over the side.

Now that I was back, no one appeared to be much interested in binge drinking. Addictions are not possible in Hell. No one here seemed to have any more than a mild psychological attraction to things. My little gang had decided to drink only once a week and keep it moderate. I was glad to hear it.

I also learned something interesting. Apparently a man named Jed had drunk three quarts of vodka and died.

"He was dead as a doornail," a girl named Brenda, who had joined the group, said. "I didn't drink that much, and when I found him he wasn't breathing. He was completely dead." She had gotten some help and moved him out of the way. They thought about tossing his body over the side, but decided they had better consult with the others. The next day there he was. Eating pancakes like nothing had happened.

"That was the weird thing," Biscuit said. "When we woke up in the morning, we all felt great. No hangover, nothing. It was like the day was just as new as our first day here. It's strange here. I wouldn't mind a smoke or another drink, but I don't need a smoke or a drink like I did on earth. All those cravings are controllable."

I was a bit of a celebrity. I had traveled thousands of miles, and everyone wanted to hear my story. The infuriating thing was, there was really nothing to tell. Yes, it's the same as it is here. The people are all white, speak English, and seem to be pretty much the same as us. For a thousand miles, I found everything along the way was the same as here. There were people living as far down and as far up I as I could see, and it never changed.

One man, a newcomer I did not recognize, said, "There's only one thing that explains it — the rest of you aren't real — mere creations like the books. My soul is probably in a vat somewhere being pumped full of sensations. You, you, and you," he said, pointing at three of us, "are nothing more than input signals to a single consciousness swimming in a God-created void."

We looked at one another and nodded. We could not refute it, but I knew I was real and assumed everyone else there was too. We turned away from him.

One young man paused and started asking me about the density of the people in the side rooms. "How many people were staying in the rooms as you traveled along?"

"About the same as here, three or four people in a room, about three empty beds everywhere I went," I answered.

"It seems strange," he said, the lines in his forehead narrowing. "Why do you suppose they didn't try to pack us in more, or spread us out more? Why a density of three or four?"

A woman named Betty seemed genuinely depressed. "A thousand miles of books? How many are here? This is going to take forever. I've looked through thousands of books already and I haven't even found a single phrase like Biscuit's 'sack it.' How are we supposed to find a whole life story?"

Betty struck me as pretty, with long, straight red

hair that fell around her shoulders. Her youth drew me in a way that surprised and delighted me. I was in a bit of a tizzy. I'd only been away from my wife for a month, but I felt a strong attraction to Betty. Although sexual in part, it seemed purer than that. I did not remember her from before I left on my run.

I answered a few more questions about my trip. I think everyone was surprised I did not find the hall's end, that I gave up after going so far, and that it was all the same wherever we went. A couple of fellows from downstairs who had come up to hear about my trip were downright hostile and implied I had made the whole story up.

"Go yourself," I shrugged at them, and they said bitterly they would. I think everyone was a little disappointed that the size of this Hell was much bigger than people imagined.

As we began to scatter to our own kiosks, I asked Betty if she was eating alone, and if so, could I join her. She seemed sort of surprised at my request, but pleasantly consented to join me for a meal. We walked awkwardly over to the kiosk.

"What would you like?" I asked innocently.

She seemed amused. "Is this a date?"

I stammered and muttered something about being a married man.

"Look at the sign on the wall. You're not married anymore," she said, grinning from ear to ear. She looked radiant, like an angel, or a Greek goddess. I just stared at her.

"Oh yeah," I mumbled, but she was taking my breath away with every word she said. I had to quit looking at her. I knew I was staring and was embarrassed and ashamed. I couldn't help it.

"I'll take a tuna salad," she finally said, adding, "with romaine lettuce."

I ordered for her and passed the salad to her as it came out of the device. I asked for fish and chips, and we carried our plates over to the middle of the nearest row of books and sat down with our legs dangling over the side. We ate in silence for a few bites, making a comment or two on how good the food was here in Hell. She was curious about me and I chattered away until we finished the ice cream sundaes we had ordered after tossing the remnants of our meals over the side. I told her about my Mormon mission in Maine. I told her about getting my master's degree in geology. I told her about raising my children, and of course I told her about my dying.

She was a polite listener and paused occasionally to ask me questions about this or that aspect of my narrative.

Finally, I asked her about herself. She looked at me shyly. "I don't know how to tell my life. It was sometimes a good life, sometimes it was not — mostly not. I grew up poor in Mississippi, near Tupelo not far from the banks of the big river. My father was nothing but hate embodied. He hated my mama. He hated me and my sister. He hated my brother most of all. He weren't the kind to beat or mistreat us, but he never said a kind word when a miserable one would do. He didn't even shout much. Just ignored us. Now, Mama he would beat. She was a small woman and if things weren't the way he liked them he would take her over his knee like she was a child and beat her black and blue with a belt.

"One day we woke up and papa was gone. Just like that. One day he just didn't come down for breakfast, and that was that. Mama never said a word where he went, but just went on with her work, washing clothes for folk like nothing had changed. She did sing a bit more after he was gone, but that was about it.

"In high school I got pregnant with my history teacher's child. He wanted nothing to do with it and told me he would kill me and the baby if I told whose it was, so I never did. The baby got taken away shortly after it was born because I kept writing bad checks. So they took the baby and put him up for adoption. I was in prison for only six months but when I got out no one would tell me where my baby was.

"So about then the war was starting, and I heard there were jobs up North for women, so I headed up there. There I met my husband of fifty-two years. The best man on earth. As good and kind as my papa was mean. We raised four daughters and a boy. All of them went on to college; every one of the girls became nurses, and the boy came back to take over my husband's lumber mill. My husband never had a sick day in his life, and when he died I thought my guts had been ripped out and thrown under a herd of buffalo. I thought I could never live or love again.

But I did. I outlived two more husbands. Good men both, but no equal to my Jonathan . . ."

She trailed off, and I was silent awhile. My lust seemed to have disappeared as she became a real person and not just a red-headed object with a nice face. I still was not used to the incongruity of this twenty-something young lady next to me talking like a ninety-eight-year-old great-grandmother.

"Do you ever think about meeting him here in Hell?" I asked. She looked at me with large wet eyes and nodded.

"Me too," I said. "I think any day she'll come walking up to me and say, 'Hi babe,' and . . ." I let it go.

We sat awhile stirring our sundaes and then threw the dishes into the hole. We knew if we left them out in the morning they would be gone, so why not enjoy the thrill of watching them fall into nothingness?

I spent my first two years in Hell with Betty. We had a fun time, but it turned out that other than our night activities we did not have much in common.

It took a couple of months before we were both convinced there were no rules about sexual activities in Hell and our spouses were not going to show up out of the blue. It was hard to start a sexual relationship in circumstances of such bizarre uncertainty, especially for an active Mormon and a good Christian, both lost in a Zoroastrian Hell. We were like virgin newlyweds. All my life I'd been raised to believe this kind of thing was wrong. All my life I had lived with a strong sense of morality. How do you give it up? How do you do things you thought you'd never do? Where do all the things you believed go, when all the supporting structure is found to be a myth? How do you know how or on what to take a moral stand, how do you behave when it turns out there are no cosmic rules, no categorical imperatives? It was difficult. So tricky to untangle. I still remember the deep sense of loss. The pain almost killed me. If it hadn't been for Betty I might have jumped—but then where would I go? I now know, of course.

3

YEAR 102:
THE MOST SIGNIFICANT TEXT

MASTER TREACLE CALLED THE MEETING TO ORDER. AS Professor of Geology, I had a seat on the fifth row and could see him standing tall on the stage of stacked books, smiling brightly in his purple robe — dyed with grape juice. A few curious onlookers from the barbarous other side of the chasm were shouting rude remarks, but as always, we ignored them. I turned around and looked at my bedmate Sandra, who was a few rows back— Assistant Professor of Calculus. She gave me a smile, looked at Treacle, and rolled her eyes. I smiled back and nodded.

Treacle cleared his throat as a signal we were to quiet down and attend.

"We will begin with a musical number by our university music ensemble." As he said this he cast a scowl my way. I was supposed to play this morning, but my turkey-bone flute had been CU-ed (cleaned up) last night and I had not had time to carve another. Apparently it came loose from the strap around my leg where I had bound it. It was a shame because I had managed to hold on to it for over a year. Oh well, *c'est la vie*.

The music was lovely, and I did feel a tinge of guilt that I was not there. I was also a little disappointed that the flutes sounded so strong without me. By ordering raw intestines to eat, several types of harps had been created by stretching the gut between the bookcases and the railing, or up and down the railing. It took most of the morning to set these instruments up, so the music they created was well appreciated. Even the barbarians in the stacks across the gap stopped heckling us while the musicians played.

After a loud and appreciative applause, Treacle stood again.

"Our invocation to the great God of Zoroastrianism will be offered by Professor Donaldson. After her prayer, this year's Most Significant Text will be read by Dr. Rachel Hasnick. Dr. Carter will introduce the text with an award presented to Stew Sand who found the text three months ago on level minus fifty-six in row five, book forty-eight, in area minus three hundred eighty-eight. There were a number of entries that might have been contenders for the MST, but when this one was found there was no question of this year's winner."

Professor Donaldson stood and raised his hands into the air.

"Great God, whose heaven we eagerly await. We are gathered here on the first day of the one hundred and second year of our time in Hell, to praise you and to honor your memory and presence. Bless these proceedings that we may find favor in your sight. That we may be led to our life stories. That the days of our imprisonment may be short. Bless our efforts. May peace be had in all our districts. May the search be undeterred. Bless our university that it may continue to prosper. That its leaders and councils may be wise in teaching truth to the inhabitants of Hell. May we be led to be better people by combining our knowledge and teaching one another the truths gleaned from our lives while on earth. May ..."

About here I faded out and snuck a peek at Sandra, who seemed to be sincerely participating in the prayer. While I would never admit it to the administrators of the university, I was more than skeptical about trying to pray. What kind of God lets demons choose such a bizarre Hell? Why put conscious beings through this? What purpose could it serve him or us? Was he/she/it worthy of worship? I honestly didn't know.

Stew, the finder of this year's Most Significant Text, was introduced and given an award (a piece of soap from the showers carved into an amazing replica of a chicken, which had been placed in a nest of coconut fiber — it is impresssive what you can get out of the food kiosks. Apparently, if it is possible to eat, you can ask for it).

Rachel got up to read the text. She was a good friend, and we had spent many a day in long talks and thoughtful conversation about the nature of life, reality, and the implications of this afterlife. She had been the editor of a literary magazine before Hell and now held a post in the philosophy group as Professor of Hell Studies. She received the book she was handed with great solemnity. She opened it. "Reading from page eighty-seven, I quote, 'The bat housed again four leaves of it.'" There was a deep silence as people pondered the significance of this passage. Barbara handed the book to Professor Treacle, who continued.

"First, note that the text is a complete sentence. Significantly, it begins with a capitalized article and ends in a period. Notice the subject, 'bat,' and the verb 'housed' refers to 'four leaves,' and we find out that they belong to 'of it.' Never before have we found such a perfect example of a complex sentence. Stew Sand is to be highly praised for finding this year's Most Significant Text. Its location has been memorized by all here, and I think there will be many who will want to visit the site of this book and ponder its meaning. Thank you again, Stew." Treacle turned toward him and with a slight bow of his head, began to clap politely. We all joined in.

Johannas Back, a food scientist, turned to me as we clapped and whispered to me sardonically, "I know exactly what it means, and I don't have to ponder it much —it means it's going to be a thousand years before we find a paragraph that makes as much sense as this stupid sentence." I laughed and nodded. But inside, of course, it disheartened me. We'd been here over a hundred years. And that was the most significant text this year? Last year's was worse—"Can dye dogs riverward."

Everyone was abuzz about how this year's sentence started with an article, had a great verb, and even seemed to make a little sense. But it made me realize it would be a long time before we found anyone's story, let alone mine.

The proceedings over, the people began to disband. A few had come from a long way. Some from as far down as the −12,853th floor and some as far away as 22,889 shelves over. The university was well thought of, and people knew its reputation even a great distance from its origin. I felt blessed to be on the faculty. I saw Rachel standing by herself holding the book she had just read from.

"Hi. Nice reading," I said as she looked up.

"Thanks," she said, smiling slightly. "Another year down and another significant find."

I gave a soft laugh—more like an audible smirk.

"Always the unbeliever, eh?" she said.

"It's just been so long — over two of my lifetimes on earth," I replied, feeling sorry for myself. "And I've found one coherent phrase in that time, 'lightbulb ocean left,' of all things ..."

She smiled. "Ah, yes, the MST of '25."

"Exactly," I continued, "and I've not found a thing since — that was a nice sentence today, by the way, but Stew's a digger, he spends most of the day with his face in the books scanning. I can't scan more than an hour or so before I just can't stand it anymore."

"Yeah, me neither."

We stood in silence for a moment, and I asked if I

could see the text. It had been in Stew's possession for most of the time and he had just given it up a week ago.

She nodded and handed me the book. I opened to the page and stared at the text. A thrill ran down me as I saw those words embedded in a sea of gibberish. Real words, with meaning, as if they had been in a sentence from a real book printed long ago on earth. I looked at it a long while, enjoying the feel of the book's weight and the deep satisfaction of finding an island of sensible text in an ocean of meaninglessness.

"It does bring a modicum of hope."

"Yes, it does ... and maybe some despair."

I looked at Rachel. Since we were all white, little differences were magnified, and her freckles made her seem different and mysterious in a way that almost intimidated me. I knew what despair she was talking about. This tiny nonsensical sentence was all that a group of over seventy-five people could show for a hundred years of effort.

She continued, "And I'm so sick of this. I'm sick of the monotony. I'm sick of this university. I'm sick of listening to people's life stories. I'm sick of listening to people repeating books they read when they were alive." Her eyes were starting to water. "And do you know what I hate most of all?"

"What?" I said as sympathetically as I could, but I could guess what was coming.

"I'm sick of having nothing to look forward to. I'm sick of not having any dreams. I've spent a hundred years — four times my earthly life — looking for a book that exists somewhere in an infinity of gibberish. I can't do it anymore. I'm sick of it." She suddenly kicked the kiosk as hard as she could, and then she melted down beside it, crying.

I just stood there for a moment. Such breakdowns were common. We were all sick of it. If I let it get to me, let it get away from me at all, I could be in the same state in a matter of minutes. I knelt beside her and lifted her up. I found tears running down my face. It surprised me. Something about the day — reading the damn text, and making such a big deal about something so stupid, had raised my feelings to the surface too.

She looked at me, noticed I was crying too, and smiled. "Bad day."

"Bad day," I agreed. I helped her to her feet, and she took a step and winced in pain.

"I think I broke my toe," she laughed wryly.

"Probably," I said. "You kicked that thing pretty hard. It will be healed in the morning."

"Yeah. Of course."

She looked around. There was still a good crowd of people around. Sandra was looking my direction. Wondering, I could tell, whether I was going to join her for dinner or keep talking to Rachel all evening. Sandra and I had been bunking together for about three years. I liked Sandra, we had a great deal in common, and I was going to miss her. It seemed funny at the time that I would think that right then, but I knew it was true. I could tell something big was about to happen. I'm not sure how I knew, but I did.

Rachel glanced at the direction I was looking and said, "You'd better go. Sandra's got a jealous streak I can feel from here. I'll be all right. Go on. I'm fine."

I ignored her. "You were on the exploration of '58, weren't you?"

"I was."

"Tell me about it," I said, with Sandra still glaring at me from the distance. "I don't think I've ever heard your version."

She gave me a grateful look and began, "Well, as you know there were eight of us. Dr. Cummings spearheaded the whole thing. He put together the four teams of eight who were to travel up, down, left, and right until we came to the end of the hall, or to the bottom floor or the top floor, but the idea was none of us would return until we found an end, even if it took twenty years ... Are you sure you want to hear this? It's not a very interesting story."

I nodded vigorously.

"Well, I was on the team with Cassandra ..."

"The anthropologist, right?"

"No, she's the Marxist economist."

"Right. Go on."

"And Jed, Conrad, Katrina, Daphne — the tall Daphne with blond hair — Mike, Rudy, and Doc."

I nodded at the familiar names.

"We went left. Every day we would walk until noon, eat something, and walk on until it was time to spend the night. After about a month, we started running into people who hadn't heard of our university. But they were always eager for news from far away. Never any diversity, of course. No old people. No children. No blacks. No Asians. No Hispanics. Just bland, ever-present whites. Things seemed civil everywhere we went — unlike the barbaric behavior and rape gangs across the divide. Strangely, after about six months the people started getting scarce. And a week after that they disappeared completely. We were alone. The books continued. The sleeping rooms continued on the same interval we had always seen them, but no people.

"At first it was pleasurable. We frolicked like kids in some secret place, but after a month we began to feel lonely. After a year, we really had nothing to say to each other, and we were on each other's nerves so badly we started sleeping in separate rooms at night. But we had our charge, and on and on we walked. We walked a year further and never said a word to each other. The following year the girls banded together and talked from time to time. The year after, a few romances and occasional conversations continued. It was on the anniversary of our fifth year that we suddenly just stopped. No one said anything. We just stopped walking, looked at each other, and turned around and came home. I can't tell you what it was like to find people again. I think the first man we ran into thought we were off our rocker, but it had been over nine years since we had seen another face, and we couldn't leave him alone. I'm sure he felt like a celebrity with all of us fawning over him. Nine years with only eight faces. It was horrible."

She fell into a thoughtful silence.

I said, "I've heard the same from the people who went up and down. After a while people disappeared, but the books went on and on ... Weren't the up group gone for twenty-five years?"

"Twenty-three, but who's counting?"

"And one never came back? Julia Hatch, wasn't it? I knew her a little."

"I think so. They said when they finally turned around she just said, 'Not me,' and kept on climbing. I wonder if she's still climbing."

I noticed Sandra was really scowling at me now. I knew in a moment she would storm off. But I just wanted to talk to Rachel.

She noticed Sandra too.

"You'd better go. She's not very happy."

I shook my head and lowered my voice. "Do you think this is really a Zoroastrian Hell?"

"Ah. Our resident non-believer. How can you doubt it? We were all told the same story by a great demon. There's a sign posted every fifty yards that tells us it is. And I don't see any way around the reality of being here. We all wake up to the same set of rules, the same consistency. Why do you doubt?"

"I don't really doubt — I just want to. I think in part it's the lack of diversity, the lack of nuance, like the veins of a leaf, or the grains in a piece of feldspar, the lack of variety and detail. I keep wondering about the idealist's perspective that our minds are sitting in a jar somewhere and all this is just a projection of some sort.

That kind of input would be easier to maintain if you didn't have to worry about detailing a dragonfly's wing."

"Do you believe that's the case? That only you are real?" Rachel asked slyly.

I sighed, "No. Not really. I can't take solipsism seriously." I smiled at her and added, "At least I know you're real."

She gave me a big smile, amused at my maudlin pronouncement, but glanced quickly over to where Sandra had been standing.

Sandra was gone. I was glad. It seemed funny that one day I would go to bed in her arms and the next not feel anything, like a switch had gone off. But no, that wasn't honest either. This had been building for a long time. Our silences were getting longer. Our arguments more frequent. How do you stay with someone when there are no dreams to build? No purpose to accomplish? No meaning? No meaning — that was the monster that drove us away from one another in the end. Always.

"People keep telling me God is good," I said, "that we need to pray every day for His kind mercy. But why pray? Everything is given to us. For protection? Why? Even if we die, we just wake up the next morning as if nothing had ever happened. Will praying hasten the search? I've seen no evidence of that. Why thank this God who has condemned us to an endless Hell? We are all slowly going crazy. And the task? We all know it's impossible. A book on our life? There must be billions of such books. In what detail? From whose perspective? A book on every second of our life would take volumes. A book about my life from my own perspective would be very different from that of an observer who loved me, or from one who hated me. Which book is the right one?" I was venting, but I could not seem to stop. So many irritations in this place, so many endless, meaningless frustrations.

"So I don't want to believe," I went on. "During my earth life, I believed I would live with my precious wife forever. I believed I would one day be a God. I believed in doing good to my neighbor. I did my home teaching. I paid my tithing. I served in my calling in church. That God made more sense than this ever could, and yet do I wake up in the Celestial Kingdom surrounded by my departed family and friends? No, I find myself on a folding chair in the office of some demon sitting behind a desk with a vision of people burning in Hell in the window behind him. So all my beliefs disappeared then. Why should I trust things now? Who knows, maybe in a hundred billion years I'll find my book. I'll stick it in the slot and boom, I'll find out that, no, Zoroastrianism isn't the truth either, but it was really the Baptists who were right all along and this is just part of God's preliminary salvo into an eternity of horrors. So it's bam, splash, and I find myself in a sea of boiling sulfur. Or maybe this is some strange philosopher's Hell where we have to experience every possible Hell that can or has ever been expressed." I sat down, frustrated and depressed. "So ... I guess I don't have much hope that things are going to get better."

She knelt down beside me and took my hands in

hers. She didn't say anything; there was really nothing to say, I suppose. Tomorrow would come, we would discuss something, eat from the kiosk, and go to sleep.

She looked at me thoughtfully, smiling sadly to herself. "I remember when I first got here, I was a vegetarian deeply committed to eating low on the food chain. When I was alive, I didn't want to be part of the industrial food complex with its abject animal cruelty. Then one day someone watching me eat said, 'What, do you think there's some Hell somewhere in the larger universe where people are running a chicken factory? Another where they make these meals for the kiosk and send them here on some sort of conveyer belt?' The absurdity of it has never left me. We can't care about anything here. We can't make a difference — all meaning has been subtracted, we don't know where anything comes from or where it goes. There's no context for our lives. We're all white, equal ciphers, instances of the same absurdity repeated over and over. We try to scratch some hope or meaning out of it with our university, but ultimately there is nothing to attach meaning to. We're damned."

She said this coldly, without complaint, staring at her hands, then added, "Well, at least I can enjoy a steak. I'm pretty sure it has nothing to do with a cow. How could it?"

I nodded and reached out and took her hand. It was slightly cool, but its physicality was real and soft. I gently rubbed her fingers and massaged her palm with my thumb. I felt her relax and sigh. No cows, no chickens, no pigs were connected with our food, of that I was sure, too. There was no life here. Hell was a machine. Except us. Here, her hand in mine was the one reality that severed us from the cold click-clack of Hell. I rubbed her hand and she sighed; wasn't that meaning? Wasn't that something we could cling to? I could *be* with this other. I could form no other relation, but maybe her hand in mine was enough, both sufficient and necessary. In Hell there was no sense of place, because all places were the same. Uniform monotony. A place without place. A place without context. But, here, now, I could rub her hand and she would sigh. She was a difference. Perhaps each person was the only difference in all these halls of unchanging ranks of books, kiosks, clocks, and carpet, and that, and that, at least, we had to hold to.

I noticed we were alone. Someone had just said another sentence had been found about a hundred floors up, and everyone had made a dash up to see it.

She looked at me. "Do you want to go up and see the text? Maybe it will make up for today's disappointment."

I did not let go of her hand.

"Rachel, you can go if you want ..." I never got to finish, because she kissed me. The deepest, most satisfying kiss I'd experienced in a hundred years. We never did find out what that text was.

Have you ever loved someone for a thousand years? I would have bet it impossible, but that's how long we were together. A thousand years we traveled the halls of Hell together. I don't remember fighting. She was magic.

Nights were wondrous. Days full of laughter and long, slow conversations. Once for fifty years we discussed dogs and decided to spend a few years pretending we were dogs, running on all fours and eating only dog food out of a dish, or occasionally gnawing on a meaty bone. Oddly enough, it caught on and several people joined our pack. We pulled the mattresses down off the beds with our teeth and slept on the floor.

In our 708th year together, we started an elaborate game of tag that involved hundreds of people and lasted for over twelve years. We developed a series of complex strategies for freeing prisoners and gaining allies when we were It — and we were always It together. We were a team, Rachel and I. Oh, I miss her so much. I think our love could have lasted forever. I'm sure it would have. She was so . . . no, I won't cheapen it by trying to express it in words and short sentences. I loved her. That is enough.

4

YEAR 1145: THE GREAT LOSS

THINGS STARTED TO FALL APART WHEN DIRE DAN, "THE prophet of doom and truth," grew in popularity and established a following of several ten thousand men and a handful of women. He claimed to be from the other side of the divide and to have been visited by God himself. God appeared in his room at night and bade him rise and hear the truth. This is how his conversation with God went:

GOD. Kneel before me, slime. Hell dweller. Stink in the nostrils of the Great God who holds in his hands your extinction. Kneel, less than a worm. Tremble, smudge on existence, twisted and unholy scab.

DIRE DAN. Speak, O Great One. I am your servant.

GOD. You are no servant of mine, puss of gall. You are less to me than the half remains of a worm discarded in a bird's unfinished meal, left in a gutter to dry, rot, and stink. Do not bother me with cries of "servant," nor speak useless flatteries in my ear.

DIRE DAN. Yes, Lord.

GOD. But I will make you a tool. Those in this Hell must be taught who it is they have offended in their sin. They must be made to feel my wrath. The time has come that they are to be scourged. You will be like a whip in my hand. You will be the sword in my clenched fist. You will bring them to punishment. The days of this peace in Hell are ended. Kill them again and again. Rape them, torture them, cause them pain and fire. Leave not a moment of peace. Teach them the wrath born of their sins and rebellions. Strike them when they are awake. Smite them when they are asleep. Cut without mercy. Slice without pity. The day is now. Teach them the horrors of a just God!

DIRE DAN. It will be done.

And so the Direites spread like a pestilence. Their numbers increased under the promise of a bright heaven to come when they had scourged Hell to the utmost. Their numbers swelled to thousands in a year. They made recruits across the gulf, on both sides of the library. Never before had we seen such terror. They hunted in packs of ten to thirty men and occasionally a few women. They were bound by oaths to cause as much hurt as they could. If you did not join, they would keep you prisoner for days. Engaging in torture. I will not describe it. It is beyond my ability. We became like animals. We ran. Hiding. Running. Watching both sides of the library, for the two sides worked together to hunt us down. We just wanted to travel to where there were no people, but the Direites kept the borders of the four directions carefully guarded.

One day, in this time of terror, two people popped out of one of the stairwells near where we were enjoying a meal. Their faces were stretched in unmistakable terror. They looked at us and screamed, "Run!"

We knew why. We did not need any other warning. Rachel and I bolted. We ran to the left as fast as we could. We could see across the divide that the Direites on the other side were directing the pack on our side to our location. We ran faster, our legs pumping like sprinters'. Suddenly, in front of us a gang poured out of a stairwell. We ground to a halt and turned the other way, sprinted into another nearby stairwell, and headed down. We flew down the stairs with the animals panting hot behind us like wolves. We raced down to another level and went right. We should have gone left. If I had one wish to make in this eternity of madness, if I could have one prayer answered in this empty place, it would be that we had turned left instead of right. Why? *Why?* has been my question ever since.

We were surrounded. Another gang poured out of the stairwell in front of us, and we were surrounded. Their eyes were terrible, their countenances radiating nothing but fierceness and hatred. They moved slowly toward us, armed with clubs and spears made of cow and water buffalo bones.

Rachel turned to me. She seemed surprisingly calm. "I love you," she said, a beautiful smile on her face.

Then she climbed up the railing and jumped. Several arms reached out to stop her, to hold her back, but they were too late. Many arms grabbed me, however, and held me fast against the railing. I watched her fall. She did not scream, she just fell downward, down, down, and down. The Direites all watched with gleeful cheers and laughter as she got smaller and smaller, until as an infinitesimal dot she merged with the ever-present vanishing point and winked out of my existence. My only joy was gone.

"I love you too," I said to the empty air below me. I was hit over the head with a bone and saw nothing but blackness.

WHEN I WOKE up, I noticed I had been moved and was looking under one of the beds in a sleeping room. Then I felt a sharp pain, and everything went black again. I woke up again, noticed the same perspective I'd seen before, heard a whistle of something swinging through the air like a baseball bat, and darkness again. This continued for thirty-seven days, which for me lasted only a few seconds.

Thinking in bits and pieces over the course of more than a month was new to me, but time and practice brought increased efficiency of thought. I had about six seconds before I was clubbed. About two of which was spent in orienting myself by recalling where I was in the thinking process, then with the remaining four I deliberated on my situation. Of course to me, the month passed in only three minutes of consciousness, but during that three minutes I hatched a plan and reached a point where I was ready to execute it.

Upon awakening, I rolled as quickly as I could in the direction away from my invisible attacker. Then, having secured some distance between me and my attacker, I rolled and leapt to my feet, and turned quickly to face my assailant. He was clubbing down with a large cow thighbone and was startled to find me gone.

I was not surprised to find myself in one of the small rooms next to a bed, but here sat my assailant, rubbing his eyes.

"Well, well, well, you got away. At least I beat Higgins's record, but not even close to Barley's." The man stood up and looked at me.

"Want some coffee?"

There were a few other people getting up, a few going to the bathrooms, and some making their way out to the kiosk. I suddenly noticed that near every bed was a crumpled body, lying still, its head bashed in and fresh blood pooling on the floor. I felt sick at the sight. What were these people doing?

"Maybe some orange juice," I said suspiciously.

At that the man shrugged and motioned for me to go out to the kiosk.

"Don't try to get away," he cautioned. "You're a slave."

"A slave?" I asked.

"Indeed, you've been adopted by the brotherhood. You will serve us, or you will be used as a morning sacrifice—as you have for the past month. As the master teaches, 'To murder a sinner in the morning is the start of a blessed day.'"

I was speechless.

"There's a chance to escape both these fates, and that is to join us and undertake the oath. One of the teachers will instruct you with the other Arisers this morning after breakfast. Go grab something for breakfast." And with that he marched into the bathroom. I stood there, stunned.

Death lay all around me, but those still living seemed not to care. They stepped and maneuvered around the many bodies like it was a normal morning. I walked out of the room and came up to the kiosk and ordered an orange juice. Bodies were everywhere. People were crumbled in the hallway. Fresh pools of blood seeped under many of the twisted bodies. I saw one man being beaten by several others. They beat him until he fell to the ground, where they kicked him until he was dead. There seemed to be no malice in their actions. It was as if they were almost bored, going through a morning ritual that needed to be done, like brushing their hair or ordering a meal from the kiosk.

I walked over to the railing and peered over, thinking of Rachel's last jump, which for me had only been a few minutes ago, but I knew in reality had been weeks ago. A wave of sadness and loss spread over me just as a voice said,

"Don't think about jumping. We'll catch you before you get a foot on the railing. Then we'll torture you in ways you would find rather unpleasant. The great thing is, every day we get to start fresh. We have people we've tortured for over a year. Great sinners, of course. They deserve it. It's God's great work."

I stared at him like he was a madman.

"You'll get used to it. Their screams, I mean. It's all God's work."

He looked uncomfortable for a moment then turned away. He stood in silence for a minute and then turned to me again.

"Let's go."

He led me to a stairway. I was seated on one of the steps that led upward with about four other men. I had not seen any women yet, but I'd heard some Direites were women. Not many, but a few.

A man came in and stood in front of us, his back to the hallway. He looked no different than any of us, with the same haircut and clothes we all had. I could not tell if he was a prisoner or a captor until he proclaimed, "I am Dire Dan."

My blood ran cold. My stomach lurched into my throat, and I felt as if I were choking. Here was the man who had caused years of pain and suffering to thousands. Here was the man who had forced Rachel into the chasm. Here in front of me, only a few feet away, was the man of my worst nightmares. My fists clenched, as rage boiled inside me.

"Listen to my words and be saved from this place.

Ignore me and you will suffer beyond anything you thought possible. I am God's mace. I am his calipers, his judgment..."

I will not sicken you with all his words. He was arrogant, full of his own importance. He could speak of nothing but his glory in the world to come. It was mad. Was madness possible here? Apparently.

When he finished he said, smiling, "Here is the decision you must make. You can join us and inflict pain and suffering, or ..." and he let the moment hang, "you can be one of those upon whom suffering is inflicted.

"If you do join us, you will be assigned a client, someone who has refused the offer you now receive. To your charge you must make this place a Hell to the fullest ability of your pathetic power. You must convince me you have made this sinner suffer to the greatest extent of your abilities. Don't worry, you will be trained..."

He droned on, but behind him the two guards standing beside him left for a moment. From the stairs on which I was sitting, I could hear screaming in the hall, and the two guards bracketing Dire Dan had first turned to watch, and then walked toward the commotion —leaving no one between Dire Dan and the landing, the hall, and the railing. I did not hesitate. I had never been filled with such a sense of rage and vengeance. He had taken Rachel. He had tortured my friends. He had destroyed our peace. All of this rationalization occurred later. In that second that I saw the clear shot, I did not hesitate. My month of learning how to think in the few seconds after awakening in the morning served me well at that instant. I leaped from the step and with the speed of a linebacker picked up the low creature with all the strength born of Rachel's loss and launched us both over the railing.

I had him around the waist and did not let go as we tumbled into the great divide between the two walls of books. He was kicking frantically and screaming that he would kill me. And he did. I had him around the waist, and he leaned back and grabbed my head and gave it a quick hard twist, breaking my neck.

In the morning we were still falling. I was a little disappointed, because I knew we were traveling down at about a hundred miles an hour, and I hoped that after a day and night we might have hit the bottom. The grave fear that it might be bottomless welled up in me. I suppose it was that fear that had kept so many of us from jumping before. I estimated we had traveled fifteen hundred miles, and still no bottom.

My enemy was still with me. He was about two hundred feet above me and was in a parachutist's dive, spread-eagled and looking right at me. I was still winging my hands like a chicken tossed from a barn and doing occasional flips, but he seemed in control. I suppose he had had all day to practice, while I was falling as dead and helpless as a crash-test dummy. His look was one of pure and absolute hatred. He maneuvered a little closer and started screaming at me what appeared to be a well-rehearsed speech.

"You maggot! Do you know against whom you fight? Dog! You fight against God! Against God. You . . ." He could not finish; he let out a scream of rage, folded his arms to his side, and dove straight at me, head first. I tried to flap out of the way, but whereas he seemed to be a guided missile, I was completely out of control. Our heads collided like two hollow melons.

When I awoke, it took me a long time to find him. I tried to look around, but I was still not in control, so I used his trick and spread out my arms, and found I was stabilizing. With my perfect recollection of the past, I thought of pictures I had seen of skydivers and tried to mimic the impression I had of their falls. After an hour or so I was doing quite well and could even control my direction.

Dire Dan, I finally noticed, was about three hundred yards below me. It made me sick to think when we hit the bottom I would have to deal with him there, but it also occurred to me Rachel would be there too. So would others who had been forced to jump because of this evil man's gangs. I figured when we hit I would have lots of allies.

My enemy was trying hard to spread himself out and slow his fall. He was heavy in build — more muscular than I — and apparently with less friction he had fallen a little faster. He would occasionally look at me and scream things I could not hear, but I too had learned to slow down. Through the day I started feeling pretty hungry and thirsty. We flew down, and I watched as my nemesis slowly drifted further and further away. I kept angling my arms so I was flying away from him, and we seemed to be drifting in different directions. It was a strange feeling, falling for so long. The wind roared in my ears, but there was a peace to it, a relaxing sense of freedom I'd never known before. I was enjoying it, I had to admit. Enjoying it immensely. New experiences in Hell were few and far between, and I was having a ball. Once I hit bottom, I planned to climb back up with Rachel and jump again. Floors flew by at an astonishing rate. I could see people occasionally stop and stare at me. Some looked on in pity, others in amusement, some with the expression that plagued those in Hell: boredom. I was surprised to see so many people, because I knew I had been falling a long time. Did the travelers of '52 make it this far down? How far to the bottom?

Just before the lights went out, I caught my last glimpse of Dire Dan. He was just a pinprick far, far below me, and we were separated by a great distance. As complete darkness gathered around me, I had a strange feeling of safety. I stayed awake for hours, but just before dawn, that inevitable moment through which no one in Hell has ever been able to stay awake, that strange hour when books are returned, the dead revived, and all wounds healed—I fell asleep and did not wake until the turning on of the lights.

Dire Dan was gone. I was never to see him again. Nor has anyone I have ever met since. He, like me, is lost in the library. Alone. I wonder, does he still feel he is the fist of God?

I was getting very thirsty. I was hungry too, but the thirst was the worst. Throughout the day I passed hundreds of drinking fountains and kiosks and could do nothing but watch them fly by. My mouth was parched and my tongue felt thick in my mouth. I tried to take my mind off things by practicing my flying. I found that by pulling my arms inside my smock and bowing them out under the fabric I could get pretty good control of my direction. I learned to increase or decrease my speed and get some measure of navigation, but the downward motion dominated everything I did, and even when I was getting some horizontal movement, I was still hurtling downward at an amazing rate. I remembered that in air, there was a limit to how fast you could fall because of friction. I recalled with my perfect memory that it was at around 120 miles per hour.

As the day came to a close, my thirst was unbearable. All my bones were aching. I fell asleep and dreamed of drinking. But no matter how much I drank in the dreams, the water did not seem to slake my thirst. My throat continued to ache, so I would try to drink more, but nothing would change. I woke up many times in the night so thirsty that was all I wanted. Why would God have structured this Hell such that every wound would be instantly healed in the morning, but only the kiosk would slake hunger and thirst?

The next three days were a blur. My tongue was swollen in my mouth, and all my bones ached. I thought I heard people offering me water. At one point I thought Rachel was falling beside me carrying a large pitcher of orange juice, which she was trying to pass to me, but every time I reached for it she would drift out of reach. Sleeping, dreaming, awake all became confused. I could no longer see clearly, and everything was a blur. Finally I must have died of thirst, because I woke one morning feeling great. I was not thirsty. I could have used breakfast, but was no hungrier than I usually was in the morning. It felt wonderful after so many days of misery and discomfort.

Still falling. Still flying past floors with occasional people, but they were getting sparser. Sometimes many floors would pass before I would see another group. How far down was the bottom? Shouldn't I have reached it by now?

I did not want to go through another cycle of dying of thirst. I decided to try to get back into the stacks. First I moved near the wall, putting my hands into my smock, and tried to slow myself by pushing my hands against the wall. It didn't work. I only seemed to push myself away from the wall.

I realized I was just going to have to superman onto the floor, which would require some pretty good horizontal speed because I would have to move horizontally into the eight-foot space between the railing and the ceiling of the floor above. So I had to move about two feet across during an eight-foot drop. I was moving way too fast for that, and even with my smock bowed into a wing framed by my arms I wasn't getting that much horizontal direction. But I had to try, I knew, otherwise I would never learn how.

I stretched and angled myself to try a glide. I was not doing too badly; I was flying right next to the railing, but was still falling too fast to get into that eight-foot span. I kicked out my leg nearest the railing and managed to get it inside. It hit the railing with such force that it felt like my leg had been ripped off, and sent me spinning. My leg was broken, and my femur had been torn from my hip. The tumbling did not help the pain. I had never been in that much pain in my life either on earth or in Hell. I went into shock and mercifully passed out. When I woke up later that afternoon, the pain was unbearable. I had to do something, so I maneuvered over to the railing and stuck my head out, hitting the railing as it flew past.

The next morning I felt fine. All was healed, but I was still falling. I decided I would try again. I maneuvered myself next to the railing and tried to get as much of a horizontal vector as I could. This time I had a better plan. I kicked my leg out as before, and it hit and broke again, but as I spun around, I tried to throw my arms around the railing on the next floor down. Though it felt like they too were torn from the sockets, I swung my legs around and into the space between that floor and the one below. I got them both in and was going slowly enough that I actually hung from the railing by my knees like a child on a monkey bar for a moment or two. But I was not inside the floor, and with two broken arms and a broken leg, I dropped again into my fall. I did not have to wait long, though, before I banged my head on the railing to forget the pain.

I tried the same thing again the next day, and almost got inside. If my back had not broken, I might have managed to land. The following day, by improving my horizontal direction and slowing myself down by using my arm and leg on the wall, I finally did it. I landed on the floor. I had broken both legs, both arms, and mercifully my neck. But lying there, with feeling only in my head, I could see I was on a floor. I had stopped falling. I would have danced if I had been able to feel my legs.

I passed out but woke up late in the afternoon and found a man staring at me. I could tell I was lying in a pool of blood and must have looked a sight with my arms and legs lying twisted and broken in a heap. I could not speak, but I moved my jaw.

He looked at me, clearly wondering what had happened. Then he asked kindly, "Were you beat up?"

I could answer nothing. He saw my struggles and squatted beside me. "Blink twice for no and once for yes."

I blinked once.

He scratched his head and said to himself, "How did he get into this mess? Did you do it to yourself?" he asked.

I hesitated, not sure how to answer, but blinked twice and then blinked once.

"Sort of?" he asked.

I blinked once.

I was starting to lose consciousness again, and he noticed I was starting to drift.

"Would you like me to kill you?" he asked hurriedly before I slipped away.

I managed a weak smile and blinked once.

I woke up in a bed! I just stared at the ceiling and

enjoyed the feeling of cozy security it gave me not to be falling. I was alone in the room and wondered where the man I had met yesterday had gone. I jumped out of bed and made for the kiosk. I had eggs, bacon, ham, pancakes, and a carafe of orange juice. It was marvelous. While I ate, I did not think of anything but the food and the sweet feel of liquid running down my throat. It had been so long since I'd had a chance to just sit and think. The Direites had killed me so frequently since my capture I'd forgotten what it was like to sit down to a meal and simply enjoy the pleasures of eating. After breakfast I looked around. I could not see a soul. The place was still and silent. I wondered how far I had traveled down. Miles and miles it must have been, but there was no way to know. I looked over the edge and was saddened to think I was going to have to continue my fall soon. I had to strike out for the bottom again to find Rachel. I knew she would be waiting for me at the other end of this horrible fall, and I had to find her. Still, I was not cheered at the prospect of falling again. It had been so hard to escape from the freefall that the thought of returning was unnerving.

I idled around the rest of the day, opening a few books and tossing them over the side. They were all gibberish of course, but I kept going through the motions of hunting. After a nap and a late lunch, I was startled to see a man approaching. When he got closer, I could see it was the man who had put me out of my misery yesterday.

"Hello," I called as he neared. "Thank you for helping me yesterday."

He shrugged. "I expect you'd do the same for me."

"Of course," I said and invited him to sit down by the kiosk. He was carrying a pillowcase with a book in it. He sat it carefully beside him and sat down with a sigh. He looked at me with a sidelong glance. "You're a long way from anyone else. Are you searching for the first floor too?"

I nodded vaguely. "Sort of, but I'm taking a break." I learned he had been traveling downstairs for years. It had been over three weeks since he had met anyone.

"In fact," he said, "I continued on after I had moved you to the bed, but started back this morning after thinking about your condition. What happened to you? I was afraid there might be some of those strange violent gangs about."

When I explained about my escape, fall, and attempt to get on the shelf stacks he was doubly amazed.

"I've often thought about making the jump to find the bottom. But I suppose I was never sure enough there was a bottom — you know, there always were those who said there was none."

He had never heard of the Direites, which I was glad to learn. Their influence had been so profound in my area of the library I was afraid it had spread everywhere. As I explained their views, he shook his head in wonder and sadness.

"So you're from way up there. You fell for what, seven, maybe ten days. At over a hundred twenty miles an hour. You've really covered some distance. I'm envious. That's over thirty thousand miles. Wow, and the top floor is higher than that. Who would have guessed?"

I smiled. "I thought I would have hit the bottom before this, too."

As was the custom in Hell, we exchanged accounts of our lives on earth, our adventures in Hell, and such stories as passed the time with others in this endless afterlife. At dinner he introduced me to a delicious Korean dish, made of sliced beef, dumplings, and a ginger sauce. This was a dish I would have to remind myself of on occasion.

"What book have you found?" I asked.

He smiled and pulled it out. "I found it on the seven thousand three hundred twenty-second floor down from prime," he said, which meant nothing to me as his prime was clearly not mine. He opened the book to a page he had marked with a napkin and handed it to me. I was stunned. It read,

Breath, comes to me in bursts of joy. Stones retched out bloody worms, worn red with the passing of licking patterns of salt. Why signal wu8&xxKJOPOlns;kkk;

I'd never read anything of such profound clarity in the library before. Tears rolled down my face, and I looked up at him in gratitude.

"Wonderful isn't it?" he said.

"It's two sentences that are grammatically correct! They make sense. This is the most amazing thing I've ever seen. It's poetry." I was wild with joy. I hugged the book and kissed its cover and passed it reverently, if somewhat reluctantly, back to him.

"Thank you," I said. "You've given me some hope I haven't had in a long time."

He nodded and without another word walked to the nearest stairwell and started down.

He had told me there was a large group of people about three weeks journey straight up. Entering the same stairwell he had just started down, I started up.

I had lots of time to think as I climbed up stairway after stairway, floor after floor. Mostly I thought about Rachel. I worried that after all this time she might still be falling. Or maybe she had escaped as I had, but how would I ever find her if she did? If I started falling again, I could fly past her at night and never find her again. Maybe I had already passed her? For the first time since my arrival I thought again of praying. I needed help far beyond what I could take control of, and prayer seemed the only measure I could take. But who would I pray to? This God of the Zoroastrians? A God who would send me to a place like this? What help would he be (if a *he* he was)? I didn't know. I had no way to find out.

I had a vague hope that the people thousands of miles below the groups I knew would be different from those I already knew (especially the Direites). How delighted I would be to meet someone from Africa or Asia. Someone with a different story to tell. The neverending sameness of all those I knew somehow blended with the sameness of this Hell. The same rooms, the same railings, the same kiosks, the same bedrooms with the same bathrooms, the same signs, with the same rug, and the endless stacks of books all bound with unerring sameness, seemed to match the sameness of the people, all white, all American, all died between 1939 and 2043, the same outlooks, the same haircuts, the same maddening habits. Homogeneity everywhere, endlessly stretching into an eternity of monotony.

I dared wonder if I might have come to a new part of the library. Perhaps this was where the Chinese were kept! Maybe I could meet an Arab from the fifteenth century! But I knew deep down it was not to be. The books were full of Roman letters, I reminded myself. But maybe I would find someone from Germany. But then there were no umlauts. From England? Maybe. But somehow I feared the defining point of this Hell was its unrelenting uniformity, its lack of variation from type. If there was a heaven at the end of this, it must be filled with great variety, perhaps a multiplicity of intelligent species spread across universes. Yes, heaven would be as full of difference as Hell was of sameness.

I thought of the mountains and forests I remembered from my life as I climbed. I thought of the intricate structure of an ant's cuticle. How delicate the song of a bird, nestled in the twisted branches of a towering pine, sounds spilling into the cool morning. I thought of the zippered feathers of a sparrow and of its patterned colors, the banded mottling of its breast, its tiny feet curled round the rough brown bark, cracked and furrowed, giving purchase to those tiny clawed feet. What I would have given even to see a cockroach in this place. It would be heralded as a treasure that could not be purchased with a king's ransom. To see its six legs splaying from its thorax would have been a sight worth waiting for in a line a thousand years long. Songs would be written about its delicate multi-segmented antennae. Its wings would have inspired such poetry as to make people weep for decades at its telling.

But here, deep in Hell, there was nothing to match such a wonder. Such splashes of variegation were denied us. Our attempts at music were nothing but a shadow of what we enjoyed on earth, but even more than music, we missed the natural sounds. The woosh of wind through the yellowing leaves of an oak on a cool day late in fall. The splashing of water over smooth stone in a tiny creek as it made its way down a steep mountain. Even the whistle of a train, or the screaming of a truck down the highway, would have seemed like a symphony.

The clomping of my feet climbing up the steps reminded me of the poverty of sensation we endured here. But on I climbed, dreaming of meeting a man or a woman from India who knew some songs I could not repeat ad nauseam. The ring of my feet striking the steps was becoming the summation of a sameness from which there was no escape. Nevertheless, I climbed on. And on. And on.

It took me four weeks, but at last I ran into someone. I entered the floor exhausted, wobbled to the kiosk, and asked for glass of Gatorade. The drink was ice cold, and I downed it with relish. I noticed a man sitting in the middle of the stacks just looking down into the endless emptiness of the gulf.

"Hello," I said.

He looked up, and I was shocked by the hollow sorrow on his face. His eyes were red and swollen, as if he had been crying for days, but now there was a coldness —a lostness more like — in his stricken, forsaken eyes that frightened me. He said nothing, but after looking at me blankly, he turned away and continued staring vacantly into the gulf.

I decided to leave him and retired to the sleeping room, took a shower, and went to bed. The lights were not due off for an hour or so, but climbing all day was exhausting work.

IN THE MORNING the man was still there. I ate a bowl of Cap'n Crunch and some toast, trying once again to engage the man in conversation, but he remained silent. I started up again. On about every fifth story up, I left the stairwell and peeked into the stacks, hoping I would run into more people. About ten that morning, I ran into a group of people. They were huddled in a small gathering, crying and talking in low sorrowful tones as if a great tragedy had occurred. As I approached I greeted them cautiously. One girl burst into tears. Everyone was mourning like I had never seen before in Hell.

In a place where there is no real death, I had seen pain, anger, hatred, viciousness, blazing insane maliceous rage, boredom often, frustration commonly, love, joy, contentment, excitement, sorrow over lost love, and a host of other emotions, but not this. Not this kind of

mourning. Such a striking combination of loss and un-
alloyed despair I had not seen since my life on earth.

"What's wrong?" was all I could say.

One of the men turned to me, his features a mask of
grief.

"Then you haven't heard?"

I gave a short version of my fall and landing in this
part of the library.

"You've come a long way," was his only comment.

I made some remark about my surprise that I had
not hit the bottom yet. One of the women and two of the
men burst into tears.

I looked at the man who was speaking and asked as
delicately as I could, "What happened?"

He stared at me as if I had just arrived off a boat in
a foreign land.

"Master Took finished his calculations." Again a
round of tears broke out among the gathered group.

He turned to me and said, "Maybe you should go see
him yourself. I can't talk about it anymore." His voice
cracked as he spoke, but he managed to add, "He's about
seventeen floors up. He'll tell you what's going on."

There was a stony silence as I backed away and
started climbing again. It only took me a few minutes to
dash up the seventeen floors.

I walked into the hall and was stunned by the
sorrow. People were weeping. Some seemed almost catatonic, staring into nothing, their faces a frozen rictus
empty of expression. I saw a man and asked where I
could find Mr. Took. He waved me down the hall. "Third

flat down," he said stiffly. I made my way through the
group of sorrowing souls.

Mr. Took was sitting on his bed, his head clutched in
his hands.

"Mr. Took?" I asked. He looked up. He didn't answer
at first, so I asked again.

"What?" he said coldly.

I explained I was new to the floor and was from
about thirty thousand miles up.

He shook his head and asked sarcastically, "So there
are still only white, English-speaking Americans even
up that high? I should have known. What do you want?"
He seemed distant.

I hesitated. "I was just wondering about the . . . sorrow."

He laughed at me and threw pages torn from a book
at me. The margins were cluttered with charcoal equa-
tions, scratched out using a sharpened bone and something burnt from the kiosk.

"Look at these. It will answer your question. Look at
them and weep, because they are going to tell you
exactly what it means to be in this Hell. Look! Look!"

I was frightened for a minute that he was going to
get violent, and backed away, but he just sat down on
the bed and put his head in his hands.

I picked up the paper and stared blankly at the
calculations, but I could not make heads or tails of them.

"How long did you work on this?" I asked after his
breathing had returned to normal. He lifted his head
and looked at me.

"What?"

"You've been doing this a long time?"

"I had an estimate in just a few minutes, but the exact answer has taken me awhile — I did not want to believe my guess."

"What are they, if you don't mind me asking?"

He let out a sigh. "I calculated the number of books in the library." He stopped and looked at the papers he had thrown at me.

"How many are there?" I asked. "Is there a finite number?" This was one of the most discussed questions in Hell. Our university, despite some people trained in calculus, had no one versed in probability theory. Had he really calculated the number of books, which was generally believed to be finite, but very large? I could feel my excitement growing. "How many?" I asked with a little more tension in my voice, realizing the implications of what I was asking.

"Ninety-five raised to the one million three hundred twelve thousandth power."

"That's a lot. Right?"

"You don't understand. In our old universe there were only ten raised to the seventy-eighth electrons."

"You mean there are more books in this library than there were electrons in our whole previous universe?"

"Way more." Then he added with an evil, mischievous look, "In fact, I've calculated the dimensions of the library. You say you're from thirty thousand miles up? Did you wonder when you would hit the bottom?"

I nodded slowly.

He laughed bitterly. "Well if you were somewhere near the middle of Hell, you only have ten to the one million two hundred ninety-seven thousand three hundred seventy-seventh light years to go." I'll never forget his cold laugh. "You have over a million more orders of magnitude light-years to fall than there were electrons in our old universe."

I fell back. "Rachel!" I cried out. "I'll never get to the bottom."

The man shook his head in disgust.

"Oh. You'll reach bottom," he laughed bitterly, "just not for a very, very long time."

5

THE DEEPEST ABYSS

I WANDERED FOR MANY YEARS AFTER THAT. I WAS PAR-alyzed. I knew finally that Rachel and I would never meet again, but I hoped for a hundred years I would happen upon her one day. I played it out over and over in my mind. I would one day walk up to a kiosk and there she would be, ordering the hummus falafel she was so fond of. She would see me and jump up and throw her arms around me. I would never let go. Sometimes, in my mind, I found her sitting on the floor of the library pulling books off the shelves and looking at them. Other times I pictured her falling past me, shouting out my name. I would leap over the railing and, plunging like superman, catch her at last. We would embrace and never let go. We would never let go until we hit the bottom a zillion, zillion years later. But these were not to be. I've never found her. I know she dwells somewhere in this vast library; like the book of my life, she exists somewhere. Right now she is somewhere, probably alone like me, and somewhere she is undoubtedly pulling book after book off a shelf, scanning it, and tossing it aside. She probably, like me, keeps a book or two at her side. Perhaps one contains a novel she's found, or a long and intricate poem. Maybe she has found her story and has left this Hell — no, like me through the eons, she has covered only a drop in the ocean of books that await our perusal.

It seems odd to me now that after so long I still focus on a time so brief as to be but a fraction of an instant in the time I will be here, but so powerfully has that instant rooted into me that I hold onto it with a hopeless desperation. Ages of universes pass while I look at books of nonsense, yet I think on and on of a love so far in the past it is incomprehensible to believe it was even real. What is love that it has such power? Whatever it is, it seems unlikely this God who placed me here knows anything about it. If it loved me in the least, could it inflict what it has upon me? Who can understand? Once I feared to say such things, dreading a worse punishment. But what worse fate could there be? To remember love and know it is unattainable? To know love wanders somewhere light-years and light-years distant, ever knowing it is forever out of reach? Forever hidden? So I pick up another book. Open it. See a page of random characters. Toss it over the edge. Pick up another. Repeat. Repeat. Repeat. Repeat ... on and on the dots signify. On and on I go, light-year after light-year, eon after eon ...

I wandered for hundreds of years. Climbing, descending, climbing. I made some friends, took some lovers, fought a few people, protected others. I am glad to say I never ran into another group like the evil one that took Rachel from me. Yet I was never the same. My loves did not run as deep and rarely lasted over a year or two. So one morning I jumped. There was nothing more to do but find the bottom and start the search for my story in earnest. I would have to fall an eternity of light years. So I ordered a lamb shank from the kiosk, fashioned a bone knife and tied it on my arm with a strip of cloth torn from my robe, and jumped.

For eons I fell. Every morning I awoke, plunged the knife into my neck, and awoke the next morning only to do the same again. Over and over, every day. Sometimes I would stay awake for an hour or so, but then boredom would set in and I would use the bone knife again.

Then came centuries of agonizing thought. I knew I had not even fallen a light-year yet. I had googols and googols of light-years to go. There is a despair that goes deeper than existence; it runs to the marrow of consciousness, to the seat of the soul. Could I keep living like this forever? How could I continue existing in this Hell? And yet there was no choice. Existence goes on and on here. Finite does not mean much if you can't tell any practical difference between it and infinite. Every morning the despair gripped me, a cold despair that reached inside, creating a catatonic numbness. There was a vague feeling of falling, of getting hungry and having a thirst beyond reason, but it seemed distant. Far away.

And for the first time since my arrival I lost awareness of the passing of days. Of how long I fell I still have no memory. The unforgettableness of this Hell was suspended and in this numbing madness I plummeted downward. How many eons passed I cannot guess. But coming out of this numbness was slow. I was more like a vegetable than a person — with my consciousness only a shadow of self-awareness, only a dim sense of qualia penetrated my mental haze. I ceased to think, to perceive. I was no more aware of my existence than a snail or even an amoeba might be.

Finally, slowly, I gained a measure of lucidity and decided to end my fall. It took me thirty-two attempts, but finally I woke up in the familiar halls of the library. Instinctively, still hoping for some luck, I pulled one of the books off the shelf—a splash of nonsense of course.

I turned my attention to the kiosk. I ordered potatoes and ice cream. Fairly pedestrian fare, but I was hungry.

I'm skipping details now — there is little more of interest to tell, but for the next hundred and forty-four years I wandered the stacks. I knew at some point I would begin the fall again, but for a long time I just wanted to find something. I did find this:

catch trees as windy dots

It was early in the morning when I saw someone fall past me. I was lonely. So lonely. Of course, this far down in the library I had met no one, so when I saw the body fall past me, I leapt over the railing immediately.

She was not hard to catch. She was tumbling dead, and I was rocketing down like a bullet — arms held close at my side in a head-first dive. When, after the short chase, I had her dead body in my arms, I wept like a baby. She was so beautiful! Like an angel. All day I stroked her hair and hugged her and wept with her dead in my arms. She was missing one arm and one leg. She must have been trying to get back on the stacks. She had a bone knife tied to her wrist. (Of course — how many design solutions were there to escape time's demands in this place?) I used it to cut strips of cloth from my smock and bound her to me. I secured her remaining leg to mine, then bound her torso to my waist. I hoped this would keep us from twisting away from each other when the hour before dawn stole our consciousness. I even prayed, I think.

In the morning we awoke at the same time. She stared at me for only a second before throwing her arms around me and holding on tight. I held on and wept with her. She pulled her head back and looked at me.

"Are you real?" she asked in wonder.

I could not answer. I just cried and held her closer. She responded in kind.

She tried again. "I'd given up."

I could only nod. Then I squeaked out a feeble "me too." There was no question what we meant.

Her name was Wand. Little else mattered. We did not exchange stories. We just clung to each other as only the lonely and lost damned can understand. We planned our entering the stacks very carefully. We did not want

to lose each other, so we fell for several days, working
out a plan to stay together. We discovered that by holding hands like a couple of crabs locked in combat, we
could begin to rotate. By pulling and pushing we could
engineer a spin, turning like a maple seedpod. By esca-
lating the rotating rhythm, like when you try to rise
higher and higher in a child's playground swing by
pumping your legs, we were able to spin faster and
faster.

She had had a good deal of trouble entering the
stacks from a free fall — as she tended not to have the
mass needed to crash hard enough into the side and
wrap an appendage over the railing. She'd succeeded
only twice in even coming close to breaking her fall and
she had last been killed when I found her on her 783rd
try. I thought of Rachel. How many times had she
tried?

The plan was to spin fast enough that when I let go,
she would have enough horizontal momentum to shoot
over the railing and into the stacks before she crashed. If
she failed, I would catch her and tie us together and we
would try again the next day. When she finally succeeded, I would try to crash as quickly as possible and
race up to meet her.

"It might take me a year to climb back up to you," I
said.

"I'll wait a hundred years if I have to," she said,
smiling mischievously, and kissed me hard on the mouth.

We made love twice, before making our attempt. We
had both fallen so often and so long that we were like

creatures of the air, and it seemed as natural as in a bed. For a day I glimpsed what heaven must be like.

We started spinning, ready to make our attempt at the stacks. I'd never gone so fast in my life. The library was spinning around me so quickly I thought I could not hold on any longer, but we did and we continued to pump our arms back and forth, generating more and more angular momentum. I'm not sure whether I released her or she was torn from my grasp by the centripetal force, but we flew apart. It worked too well. She flew away from me like a bullet. I hit the railing with such force I nearly lost consciousness, but luckily only broke my hip and back. To my delight as I slid away from the railing into another free fall I saw she had made it onto the stacks — first try! She was not killed either and she managed a smile from the floor of the hall as I slipped into unconsciousness.

I awoke the next morning and immediately tried crashing into the side. It was foolish to hurry and not to prepare better, and I only managed to lose an arm and consciousness. The next day I thought through my plan more carefully before executing it. I almost made it back into the stacks on the first try, but lost a bit of balance on my approach, and when I fell away could not hook my legs over the railing. I wasn't killed, so I tried again a little later in the afternoon, but was in so much pain from the morning's attempt, it was hopeless. I was getting anxious by this point; I figured I was falling about 2,880 miles a day, 62,000 flights of stairs, and every day I wasted I was adding about three months of climbing. The next day I was highly motivated and gave it all I had. I careened feet-first into the stacks. My legs caught on the bar and tore from their sockets, but it slowed me enough to be able to backflip so I could hook my arms on the next floor's railing and hold on. With a Herculean effort of will, I pulled my remaining torso over the rail.

"I'm coming, Wand," I said, beaming brightly as I died.

The next day I barreled up the stairs. I flew. I bound up two steps at a time. I was relentless. After the first month, even though I knew I had not climbed nearly high enough, I shouted her name on every floor. My every thought was of finding her, and I would run long after the lights went out, until I passed out in that strange hour before dawn when sleep can't be helped and all things are repaired and made right and new in Hell.

The days passed in a dream. I pictured our reunion again and again, played it out in my mind over and over until I'd almost worn a groove in my thoughts, so deep that it seemed the only thing I could think of was our re-union. Anticipation is a gift. Perhaps there is none great-er. Anticipation is born of hope. Indeed it is hope's finest expression. In hope's loss, however, is the greatest des-pair.

I never found her. I don't know what happened. I searched everywhere she could have been. I called her name relentlessly, but she was gone. I never found her. I continued down after a score of millennia of wandering, opening an occasional book, but mostly looking for her. Of Wand I found no trace. Now I wonder if our meeting was real. Perhaps it was a dream? Maybe my memory of her getting into the stacks was an illusion, and she plunged light-years below me. She is gone. That at least is clear.

All hope is gone also. All hope for anything has vanished — meeting a person, finding a book, discovering some hidden way out. So much time has passed, what is left to say? All variety is lost, and billions of years spent searching through books has left me a poor conversationalist. I could tell you of my fall to the bottom — the starving and dying over and over in endless cycles of pain and forgetfulness. I could tell you of starting my search in earnest from the bottom floor. Of moving slowly up light years and light years of stairs. Of opening books beyond count. I could tell you of occasionally, every eon, meeting a person, with whom I might stay for a billion years. But what of it? After a billion years there is nothing left to say, and you wander apart, uncaring in the end. The hope of a human relationship no longer carries any depth or weight for me, and all meaning has faded long ago into an endless grey nothingness. Now the search is all that matters. I know there will come a time when I find my book, but it is far in the future. And I know without doubt that it will not be today. Yet a strange hope remains. A hope that somehow, something, God, the demon, Ahura Mazda, someone, will see I'm trying. I'm really trying, and that will be enough.

APPENDIX

THE LIBRARY OF BABEL CONTAINS ALL THE BOOKS OF A certain size that can be written. I assume all the characters on a standard keyboard and that each book (as described in the original story by Jorge Luis Borges) is 410 pages long with 40 lines of 80 characters on each page. So the total number of characters in the book is:

$$410 * 40 * 30 = 1,312,000$$

With about 95 possible characters on a standard keyboard, that implies that the number of possible books is $95^{1,312,000}$, a rather large number when one considers that there are only (according to Arthur Eddington [1882–1944]) 1.5^{80} electrons in the universe. Now, assuming the books are about 1.5 inches thick and take about 1.5 feet to shelve vertically, figuring about 8 shelves 200 feet long and about 100 square feet of living space, the width and breath of the library (given two shelves, one for each side of the library) is about $7.16^{1,297,369}$ light-years wide and deep.

Made in the USA
Middletown, DE
15 January 2018